David Asher, Lazarus Geiger, Alfred Geiger

Contributions to the History of the Development of the Human Race

David Asher, Lazarus Geiger, Alfred Geiger

Contributions to the History of the Development of the Human Race

ISBN/EAN: 9783337368050

Printed in Europe, USA, Canada, Australia, Japan

Cover: Foto ©Andreas Hilbeck / pixelio.de

More available books at **www.hansebooks.com**

CONTRIBUTIONS

TO THE

HISTORY OF THE DEVELOPMENT OF THE HUMAN RACE.

LECTURES AND DISSERTATIONS

BY

LAZARUS GEIGER,

AUTHOR OF "ORIGIN AND EVOLUTION OF HUMAN SPEECH AND REASON."

Translated from the Second German Edition

BY

DAVID ASHER, Ph.D.

CORRESPONDING MEMBER OF THE BERLIN SOCIETY FOR THE STUDY OF
MODERN LANGUAGES AND LITERATURE.

LONDON:
TRÜBNER & CO., LUDGATE HILL.
1880.

TRANSLATOR'S PREFACE.

IT is a source of lively satisfaction to me to have been chosen as the medium of introducing to the English public the late lamented author of the following Lectures and Essays, one of the most original thinkers Germany has produced in recent times, and the "greatest of her philologers," as he has been styled by a competent judge. His work itself, however, will best speak for him, and needs no commendation on my part. Let me only add that, though these Lectures and Essays, now submitted to the English reader, are but "chips" from the author's "workshop," as it were, yet I believe they afford a good glimpse of his eminent powers and brilliant genius as an investigator. But a word, I feel, is needed on behalf of myself as translator. No one can be more fully alive than myself to the difficulties of translation, and hence it is not with a "light heart" that I ever undertake the task. If I have ventured to do so on this occasion, it was owing to my belief in the adage: *Amor vincit omnia.* Love of the language into which I had to translate, happened to combine, in this instance, with love of the subject and admiration of the author. From his exceedingly clear, aye, pellucid style, my difficulties have certainly been considerably lessened; still, a conscientious translation is always an arduous task, and I can only hope, conscious of having honestly striven to do justice to the original, I may have succeeded in likewise satisfying the English reader.

THE TRANSLATOR.

Leipsic, *June* 1880.

PREFACE.

———•———

IN editing the following Lectures and Dissertations
of my late brother, I have to crave the indulgence of
the public for having ventured, as a non-scientific
man, to undertake such a task. But I deem it my
duty not to withhold from the world any of the
author's investigations, and now put forth, as a first
instalment, the present pages, which the departed was
about himself to revise for the purpose of publication
when death overtook him. The first five Dissertations are a literal reprint of the Lectures as they
were delivered, and partly already published; only
in the second I have added from the MS. a passage
in brackets which had been omitted in delivery so
as not to exceed the measure of time allotted to each
speaker. The last Essay, written in 1869–70, was
intended for a scientific periodical, and was to open
a series of similar dissertations. The unremitting

endeavour which ever distinguished the author to improve and perfect his labours prevented him from sending the Essay to its destination, as he was not spared to give it a final touch.

ALFRED GEIGER.

Frankfort-on-the-Maine, *June* 1871.

CONTENTS.

I.

Language and its Importance in the History of the Development of the Human Race.

[A Lecture delivered at the Commercial Club of Frankfort-on-the-Maine, December 7, 1869.]

IN the restless activity which science displays in our times, there appears, with ever-increasing distinctness, a phenomenon which, more than any other, confers on it a noble humanity and significance: it is the inter-penetration of the practical and ideal. The period is not yet far behind us when practical and scientific labour stood apart from each other as strangers. On the one side was seen the great mass of the toiling people, who did not understand how to respect their own activity, and were almost ashamed of it; on the other, erudition, confined to a class, and often barren of any result. Occasionally there arose a lonely un-comprehended thinker, who carefully concealed himself from his contemporaries, because to be understood was almost sure to entail excommunication and death. How different is it now, when mechanical labour finds a higher reward in the elevating consciousness of having co-operated in the mighty and arduous work of rendering mankind happy than in the wages it earns,

A

and when science takes refuge in warm, feeling hearts, to share their cravings and hopes, and perhaps, too, to raise them to those heights from which she has descended!

The chemistry of our days gives us information about the air we breathe, the provisions we are to select; it teaches us how to cultivate the soil and how to produce thousands of objects of art and industry; but at the same time it lays open to us the mysterious nature of things. In decomposing before our eyes an apparently uniform body into various invisible elements, it rends the veil of outward appearance and of illusion, teaches us to doubt the evidence of our senses, and at the same time to comprehend the perpetual transformation and growth in nature. Mechanics, by means of which man's machines are built and the giant forces of heat and electricity rendered subservient to his use, at the same time put the great question to him, what light, sound, heat, and electricity are; and suggest to him a primitive power which disguises itself, as it were, in all these phenomena, appearing now as sound, now as heat, and may be finally transformed even into mechanical force, a pressure, or an impulse. Equally so the study of language, besides its practical objects known to us all, has in our days acquired an incomparable philosophical importance, seeing that it affords a key to one aspect of the world and existence which physical science could never have reached, and gives us an explanation of what we are and of what once we were, of our reason and our history.

The first commonplace object which may induce us to study languages is, in the first instance, a purely practical one. We may wish to find our way in the streets of some foreign city or learn to converse with foreigners who have come to visit us. But, however commonplace such a proficiency may be, it already touches, without our always being aware of the fact, upon a marvellous domain. We face a being which thinks as we do, but which seems by nature to be relegated to another sphere as regards its mode of expression. The strangeness of this phenomenon is felt by every one who, for the first time, hears a foreign child speak its native language or sees himself surrounded abroad by people all speaking a foreign tongue. Language seems to us so natural and human, and it seems such a matter of course that what we say should be at once understood—and now, all of a sudden, behold! there is a barrier between man and man, analogous to, though infinitely thinner than, that between man and the brute, who likewise do not understand each other by nature, and can learn to do so only very imperfectly by art. The first discovery of a people speaking a foreign language must have been attended with tremendous surprise; at least as great as the first sight of men of a different colour of the skin. In speaking a foreign tongue, therefore, we surmount in reality a barrier raised by Nature herself, and as the ocean, which, in the words of the Roman poet, was created to separate the nations, has by navigation been converted into an immense channel of communication,

the study of living languages tends to create an asso-
ciation of men out of groups of peoples scattered
about by nature. In reading distinguished authors in
a foreign language, we feel a kind of emancipation from
the narrow boundary of nationality; new spheres of
thought, new conceptions are opened up to us with
every newly unlocked literature; the peculiar forms
in which each people clothes its divinations, its love,
its scientific thought, its political hopes, and its inspi-
rations, enrich our minds; all these become ours, we
become all these. And how much greater will be our
profit if we do not content ourselves with merely
crossing the boundary line which a mountain or a
stream or an accidental circumstance in the migration
and spreading of our ancestors has drawn for our
nation, but find in language a means of penetrating
the darkness of ages, of transposing ourselves into the
past in order to communicate with the minds of
primeval times! It is no small matter to say to one's
self, "These words which I am reading, the sounds which
I am reviving with my lips, are the same as those with
which Demosthenes once called upon his native city,
ensnared by treason, to try to regain her freedom,—
the same in which Plato couched his own and his
master's lofty teachings." By the Nile on the Theban
plain there is seen a gigantic statue of King Ameno-
phis, enthroned on high—the so-called pillar of Memnon
—sixty feet high. In the days of the Roman Empire
there was heard in this statue daily at sunrise a
musical sound; all the world went on a pilgrimage to

the miraculous statue; men and women for centuries
left their names and hymns of praise expressive of
their admiration inscribed on the gigantic monument,
and told how they had beheld its stupendous size and
heard its divine song. Homer resembles this Memnon
statue. If all who have for millennia repaired to this
marvellous monument of the earliest ages of Greece
in order to listen to the sounds of the dawning of
European poetry, could have left us their names inscribed at his feet, what a catalogue it would be!

But however incalculably great is the influence which
the treasures of ancient literature have exercised and
are still exercising—thereby, at the same time, bearing
an elevating testimony to the immortality of the creations of the human mind, even beyond the life of the
language in which they are written—yet they present
another aspect which is calculated to stir our hearts,
if not more strongly, at all events more deeply. The
authors of past ages tell us a great deal that is sug-
gestive and instructive, in the same way as they im-
parted it to their compatriots, for whom they designed
it; but in doing so they, in addition, betray something
else which they could not intend at all. Involuntarily
they afford us, by a casual description, or an uninten-
tional word, that was superfluous for them but is invalu-
able to us, a picture of the life of their time; and what
results from the careful collection of all these minute
traits is the lesson that human thought and volition,
from the earliest times of which a record has come
down to us, have been subject to a mighty trans-

formation. Accordingly the writings of ancient times are no longer mere literary productions for us to enjoy, and to enjoy so much the better the nearer they come to our own time and the more congenial they are to our minds, but they are monuments which we study, and which, on the contrary, we grasp at the more eagerly the older and more alien they are to us. The consciousness of the importance of literature in this sense is of very recent date; nay, I may say it is not even now sufficiently developed. It is true the study of antiquity has been in vogue ever since the revival of learning at the beginning of the modern era, but its object was not to gain from the reports of the authors an idea of the condition of mankind in their days, but inversely to gain that knowledge of the state of antiquity which was requisite for the purpose of understanding the authors. Even down to the last century Homer was judged by the standard of poets in general. He was ranked, let us say, by the side of Tasso or Milton, in the same way as we may mention Shakespeare and Schiller together. At length F. A. Wolf came forward with the question whether Homer had had any knowledge of the art of writing, and more especially had practised it himself; and having negatived it, he argued that such extensive poems could not possibly be produced by a single person from memory. He then endeavoured to show that we have in them the work of many individual singers, who composed short detached pieces and recited them to the cithern, as the singers mentioned in Homer himself were wont to do. No doubt he had not yet found the right solution, and the question as to the origin of the Homeric poems continues even now to be discussed over and over again; but it is indubitable that the matter of these poems cannot possibly have sprung from one head. The Trojan war is not a true history dressed up by the poet, still less is it his own invention; but in reality it is, with all its details, a primitive popular belief, much older than any line of any existing epic. Achilles and Odysseus are not imaginary poetical characters, but were demigods of the Greeks in primeval times; and mythology, with all its oddities, far from being invented by the poets for the purpose of ornamenting their poetry, was, on the contrary, the sacred conviction of that primeval age. The stories of Hera struck by Zeus in his anger and suspended in the clouds, of Hephæstos, who wishes to come to the rescue of his mother, and whom Zeus seizes by the leg and flings down to the earth, where he alights in Lemnos and is picked up half dead, formed in the age of Voltaire the subject of sneering criticism; they were, in his eyes, insipid fancies, which a polite poet at the court of Louis XIV. would certainly not have indulged in. But there is no doubt that, whoever was the Homer of these and similar poems, he fervently believed in the truth of precisely such legends. They were sacred to him and his audience; they were already then ancient and not understood; they conceal some deep mysterious meaning; how and when may they have originated? Here the problem of the formation of myths, of the origin of faiths, the solution of which has only just begun, is exhibited to our view.

While an unexpected background became thus visible behind a book which thousands had read and fancied they understood, the present century has resuscitated an even remoter antiquity, and gained for the investigation of primitive times a new subject, the very extent of which alone cannot but raise astonishment, and of which our ancestors dreamt as little as of the great technical inventions of our age.

We now know monuments and writings compared with which all that formerly was regarded as most ancient, Homer and the Bible included, appears almost modern.   The French expedition to Egypt under Napoleon I. had an importance for European science similar to that which Alexander's to the East had : it gave rise to the investigation and representation of ancient Egyptian monuments, and at the same time to the discovery of that ever-memorable stone of Rosetta, which in an Egyptian and Greek inscription contained the proper nouns that led to the decipherment of the hieroglyphics.   Two discoveries, indeed, concurred in bringing about this great result. The one, already previously made, was that the language of the ancient Egyptians was substantially identical with the Coptic, still preserved in the ecclesiastical literature of the Egyptian Christians; the other is Champollion's, that the hieroglyphics were a phonetic, partly even an alphabetical, writing.   Those singular pictures, which had so long been thought

confused symbolical mysteries of priests, turned out
to be writing once accessible and intelligible to the
whole people. It was not always profound wisdom
which was hidden beneath these hieroglyphics : over
a picture representing oxen might be read the simple
words, " These are oxen." Champollion read and translated innumerable inscriptions ; he composed a grammar and a dictionary of the hieroglyphics, and
already in the first of his works, masterly both for
their style and matter, he communicated the decipherment of a quantity of names of Roman, Greek, and
national rulers of Egypt, from which an entire
history of the kingdom up to an incredibly early
period began to dawn. There appeared, composed
of hieroglyphics, the names of Alexandros, Philippos,
Berenice, Cleopatra, Tiberius, Claudius, Nero, Ves-
pasianus, Titus, Domitianus, Nerva, Trajanus, Had-
rianus, Antoninus, Diocletianus, as well as Xerxes and
Darius, Psammetichus, Shishank, and Rameses ; and
gradually there were gathered and identified from pyramids and rock-tombs, from the walls of temples and
palaces, the whole long list of names which Manetho,
a priest of the time of Ptolemæus Philadelphos, has
preserved to us—a list of thirty dynasties, to the six-
teenth of which, at the earliest, belonged the first
Pharaoh, the contemporary of Abraham, mentioned in
the Bible. The 331 names of kings which the Egyptian
priests enumerated to Herodotus from a papyrus, the
346 colossal wood-carvings of Theban high-priests
which they showed him, as they had succeeded each

other from father to son, all men and sons of men, without a single god or demigod, are no longer fables for us. All the Pharaohs have risen from their graves, and in addition to them the numberless gay pictures of a full and abundant life of the people, all ranks and all occupations being preserved with wonderful fidelity, and domestic scenes of touching truth and simplicity, three and four millennia old! No inconsiderable relics of literature, too, have been found,—documents from daily life, historical records, and poetry, and of the sacred books, especially the so-called Book of the Dead, upon which criticism has already laid its hands, trying to separate a more ancient nucleus from subsequent commentaries.

Far less important, but interesting as the solution of a problem which seemed almost impossible to be solved, is the decipherment of the Persian cunei-form writing. On a precipitate side of a rock about 1500 feet high, near Bisitun, in ancient Media, there was found, at an inaccessible height, the coloured relievo-portrait of a king, who, attended by his guards, sits in judgment upon his vanquished foes. One of them is lying prostrate, and the king sets his foot on his body; nine others are standing chained before him. This relievo is surrounded by not less than a thousand lines of cuneiform characters. Similar characters were found on the rocks of Nakhsh in Rustein, on the ruins of the palaces of Persepolis, and in other places. But neither the writing nor the language of the inscriptions was known; aye, not even an approximate guess at their contents could be made. How could hopes be entertained of their ever being read? And yet we have succeeded so completely that at this day we are able to read the Persian inscriptions with nearly the same certainty as Latin. The first successful attempts in this direction were made here at Frankfort. Professor Grotefend, since 1803 vice-principal of the grammar-school of this city, with the sagacity of genius, recognised in some briefer inscriptions, copies of which were at his command, the passages where names of kings were to be expected, and with a rare gift of combination he discovered, by a comparison of the names of the Persian rulers known to us according to their sounds and the relationships of the kings bearing these names, those of Xerxes and Darius. The latter called himself in an inscription son of Hystaspes; this, too, Grotefend recognised on finding that, in agreement with history, the title of king was absent in the case of Hystaspes. He had at once recognised in the Persian cuneiform inscriptions an alphabetic writing: from the names deciphered he traced out part of the alphabet and attempted to read entire inscriptions. Upwards of thirty years, however, elapsed ere Professor Lassen succeeded in discovering an alphabet complete in all essentials, and, the science of language having meanwhile made rapid strides, and languages which had great affinity with ancient Persian having become better known, in actually deciphering and translating the inscriptions. At present we read on the Bisitun

monument a whole history of the reign of Darius in
his own words. The man on whom the king, armed
with a bow, puts his foot, is the false Smerdis, or, in
Persian, Barthiya, known to us from Herodotus. The
inscription beneath his portrait runs thus: "This is
Gumata, the magician; he has cheated; he said: I am
Barthiya, son of Kurush. I am king."

On the sites where Nineveh and Babylon once stood
there have been quite recently, as is well known, likewise brought to light, amongst ruins of palaces and
imposing sculptures, numerous inscriptions, especially
tiles and cylinders, bearing cuneiform writing—the
only gloomy remnants of Assyrian and Babylonian
magnificence and universal empire.

Here, too, the problem was not only to decipher
unknown contents conveyed in an unknown writing, but
first to discover a language, nay, several languages, the
very existence of which had partly been unknown.
Fortunately the Assyrian language is met with on
Persian monuments too; on several of them one and
the same inscription is repeated in the Persian and
Assyrian languages; and the Persian text having once
been deciphered, it also afforded a clue to the decipherment of the Assyrian.

In order to appreciate the effect which the coming
to light of all these new and yet most ancient marvels
could not fail to produce on the conception of our time,
we need but realise the impression made by a ruin
only a few centuries old, or the excavation of an
ancient coin or utensil, or even a mere rough stone

that in olden times passed through the hands of man, and still shows traces of having done so. The curiosity raised by what we have never before seen, the desire and craving of lifting the veil from the realms of the past, and of catching a glimpse, at least, of what has for ever perished, are blended with a feeling of awe and devoutness. How peculiarly are we moved at the sight of the slightest object brought to daylight from the buried streets of Herculaneum and Pompeii; how many reminiscences it evokes! In the case of an unknown, strange antiquity, however, that suddenly begins to revive and stir before our eyes, every one feels something analogous to what we feel at the sight of the curious extinct animals of the antediluvian world—the Ichthyosauri and the Mastodons. We cast a divinatory glance at unmeasured periods of creation, and begin darkly to guess at that great mystery—the mystery of our development.

And yet it was not the treasures discovered beneath the soil which were destined to contribute most to the elucidation of that mystery.

The finding, nay, one may say, the discovery of two literatures, which were indeed defunct, but were so in no other sense than the Latin or Hebrew—that is to say, which still continue to be studied and reverenced by living peoples—this discovery, with its consequences, it was which formed an era in European conception as to the past of humanity. Both literatures were discovered in East India. Zend literature, the sacred writings of the ancient Persians, ascribed to Zoroaster, had been carried away with them to India by the Parsees, who remained faithful to the ancient religion, on their flying from their native land to save themselves from the Mahomedans. Sanskrit literature is the holy national literature of the Brahmanic Hindoos themselves. The merit of having discovered and promulgated these treasures, of which, until about the middle of last century, no European scholar had any inkling, is due, in the first instance, to the English and the French, who were at that time engaged in a mutual struggle for the possession of India. The knowledge of the Zend writings we owe before all to French, that of Sanskrit to English science. It is German scholars, however, who in a pre-eminent degree have thoroughly investigated both, and who have more especially made use of them in perfecting linguistic science. As Columbus, urged on by an irresistible impulse which made him overcome all doubts and surmount all difficulties, went in quest of the western hemisphere, so Anquetil du Perron, from 1754, searched for the celebrated writings of Zoroaster among the priests of the Parsees in India, and employed his life in translating and commenting upon them. Nothing more strikingly exhibits the contrast of our times to those than the disappointment which the writings, brought home at so much sacrifice, then caused in Europe. Of the wisdom which so great a name led to expect they contained but little. On the other hand, the god Ahuramazda occasionally revealed in them things which, from their childlike naïveté, could only call forth smiles ;

so especially the well-known passages referring to the dog, the sacred animal of the Persians, in which the mode of his keep, his punishment when he bites, his character, his treatment in illness or when not quite in his senses, and how one has to proceed if he refuses to take the medicine, are discussed with solemn gravity.

Yet the question as to the character of the people's imagination, by what motives it must have been swayed when the Persians nursed the dog with such solicitous care, or when the Egyptians built vaults at Memphis to the holy embalmed corpses of Apis, sixty-four generations thereof lying buried there, is of such importance to us, that we willingly forego the wise teachings of those times, seeing that there is no lack of such in our own days, would we but listen to them. We are here reminded of an incident communicated by Professor Max Müller touching that portion of Sanskrit literature which is the most important to us— the Vedas. A talented young German, Dr. Rosen, who died at an early age, being occupied in the rich library of the East India Company in London with copying the Veda hymns, which he commenced editing in 1838, the enlightened Brahmin, Ramahan Rai, being then in London, could not wonder enough at this undertaking: the Upanishad, he said, were of greater importance and much more deserving of publication. These, the youngest portion of the Vedas, contain a mystic philosophy in which may be found a kind of monotheism or pantheism, which seemed to the Hindoo rationalist, as to many others, the *non plus ultra* of all religious wisdom.

But in reality the primeval Veda hymns, quite pagan, naïve, and often grotesque though they are, of which the Hindoo with his modern culture may have been secretly ashamed, but in which the youth of mankind breathes with delightful freshness, are to us the true jewel of Sanskrit literature. They do not, indeed, contain a religious system available for us, but they teach us how the religion of man was developed.

The knowledge we gained of the Sanskrit language in itself, however, quite apart from its literary treasures, was perhaps productive of still greater effects. That language, notwithstanding the wide space that separates us from it, exhibited a close affinity to our European languages. There were found in it the words *pitar* father, *mâtar* mother, *bhrâtar* brother, *svasar* sister, *sunu* son, *duhitar* daughter; names of animals, such as *go* cow, *hansa* goose (German *Gans*); and numerals, such as *dvau* 2, *trajah* 3, *shaṭ* 6, *ashṭau* 8, and *nava* 9. This is quite a different relation from that existing between our language and French when we borrow from it such a word as, for instance, *Onkel*. Sanskrit has not only its vocabulary in common with German, but even the inflection: *e.g., asti ist, santi sind.* In words borrowed from the French, on the contrary—as, for instance, in *marschiren* (to march)—we retain the German inflection, and say, for instance, *ich marschire* (I march), *du marschirst* (thou marchest). In eliminating from a language all foreign words, its vocabulary indeed diminishes, but nevertheless a complete language still remains. Cognate languages, on the contrary, have so much in common that, were we to eliminate all of it, only something quite incomplete would be left. French, for instance, is closely related to Italian, and we here see quite plainly why both languages would cease to exist if they were to abstain from all the words and forms they have in common. The reason is, French was not by any means a finished language which borrowed Italian words, like German when it admitted the word *Onkel*, but the resemblance arises from the fact of French and Italian being both derived from the Latin, thus once forming a single language, viz., this very Latin. Such, too, must be exactly the case with German and Sanskrit; both must once have formed one language; only this one language, of which German and Sanskrit may be almost called the daughters, as French and Italian are of Latin, is no longer extant. We know there has been a people that spoke Latin, viz., the Romans. Equally there must have been a people that spoke the original language from which German and Sanskrit have descended, a people that existed at a time when there were as yet neither Germans nor Hindoos. Not only German, however, but Latin, Greek, Russian, and all the Slavonic languages too, as likewise the Keltic, and in Asia the Armenian and Persian, with some collateral branches, are related to Sanskrit. The ancestors of all those peoples who spoke these languages must, therefore, have constituted one people, together with the ancestors of the Germans and Hindoos, and the science of language must therefore assume a primitive people

B

much older than anything we know of in European
history. Where it had its seat is not yet determined,
still less the time at which we have still to think of its
being united. On the other hand, language affords remarkable indications by means of which we may ascer-
tain something as to that people's stage of culture.

The common prehistoric language referred to can
obviously have had words only for such objects as the
people that spoke it were acquainted with. Thus if, for
instance, *ship* in Sanskrit, as in Greek, is *naus*, in Latin
navis, a word akin to our *Naue* and *Nachen*, the Indo-
European prehistoric people must have known the ship.
Equally we find a common word for oar, but none for
sail. Vehicles must likewise have been known to
that people; of arms it knew the sword, but scarcely
the bow. In all probability the custom of painting and
tattooing it had in common with the aborigines of
America and Australia. Our word *Zeichen* (sign) is not
only connected with *zeichnen* (to design, draw), but also
with the Greek στίγμα and to stigmatise, *i.e.*, to tattoo.
The first sign, and the first design, were those which
were tattooed in the skin.

Here we have an example of the employment of
words as keys to the history of human civilisation. A
word which we use now, but which originated at an
earlier time, very often enables us to guess at the former condition of the thing which it denotes. Suppose,
e.g., we did not know what writing material preceded
our steel pen, the word *pen* would perhaps suggest to
us that it was taken from a bird. Such inferences,

indeed, lead far, very far back. If we do not limit
them to a single family of languages, but endeavour to
gather, as far as possible, all that is preserved of such
indications in the languages of the whole earth, results
will be arrived at of the utmost importance to our
knowledge of the earliest ages of mankind. In our
retrospect we finally come down to a condition which,
though superior to that of animals, is yet inferior to that
of any savage people whatever of whom history contains
a record. All human beings possess tools, and have
within the memory of man always possessed them; aye,
such possession belongs to the distinguishing characteristics of man as compared to animals. But now there
is to be traced in a great number of the words denoting
activity with tools a more ancient idea, implying an
analogous activity, but such as is carried on with
natural organs. What follows thence? I believe
nothing but that, as in modern times we have in writing
passed from the bird's feather to the metallic pen, as in
primeval times tattooing changed into drawing and writing, so at a much earlier period all cutting to pieces
was preceded by tearing. Man was at one time without tools, and in his outward mode of life differed but
little from the animal. And as it is with the outward
man, so the inner man, too, shows a strong contrast.
If we regard his moral condition, we must not, in looking at prehistoric times, ask merely whether man has
since improved, whether the passions have softened
down and crimes diminished. We find, on the contrary, and that partly down to historical times, the

notions of good and evil differing very essentially from
ours, *e.g.*, cannibalism, not merely practised out of glut-
tony or barbarism, but regarded as a downright good and
religious action.   The notions of justice at the period
when the Indian Code of Menu originated rested so
entirely on a fantastic foundation, that, according to
that code, an individual of the lower caste, for striking
a member of the higher one with a stick, was to lose
his hand, and for kicking him, his foot.   And in conformity with this, the breaking of a dyke is menaced
with the punishment of drowning.   This purely outward mode of retaliation, according to which justice is
not sought for in the due proportion between the punishment and the gravity of the offence committed, but
in a material similarity between the two, is met with
at the lowest stage of legislation among all nations.
The oldest Roman and German laws contain many such
provisions.   Thus we find in German antiquity the
chopping off of the hand as a punishment of perjury,
for no other reason than because the hand is raised in
taking the oath.   To the same category belongs the law
of retaliation (*lex talionis*), which was already known
by this name to the Roman law, and formed one of the
most ancient elements in the laws of the twelve tables.
But almost everywhere we find, as nations enter on the
stage of history, the progress already made that, under
the form of compensation and ransom, a new practice
has been substituted for the primeval formulæ, and a
changed, more developed conception of law has taken
·their place.   The Biblical "eye for eye, tooth for tooth,"

was already in ancient times interpreted to mean a corresponding fine, and the interpretation probably acted on throughout the historical period. If capital punishment appears to us at present most justified in the case of murder, we must not forget that this penalty is, after all, based only on the same principle of retaliating like for like, and therefore on a fantastic foundation.

If we examine the words, those oldest prehistoric testimonies, all moral notions contain something morally indifferent. *Gerecht* (just), *e.g.*, is only equivalent to *recht, richtig* (right) ; it is connected with *ragen, recken* (to stretch), and originally meant stretched out straight. Now Gerechtigkeis (justice), however, is not by any means likened merely to what is straight, such as we speak of straightforwardness of mind ; but, in reality, it only means the right, straight way. *Treu* and *wahr* (true) are actually equivalent to trustworthy ; still earlier they only signified firm, fortified. *Böse* (bad) we still use of what is damaged, and say bad (rotten) apples, bad (sore) fingers.

But why have not the morally good and bad their own names in the language ? Why do we borrow them from something else that had its appellation before ? Evidently because language dates from a period when a moral judgment, a knowledge of good and evil, had not yet dawned in man's mind.

And as regards the intellectual condition of man, it must likewise have once been incredibly low. Thus it is not to be doubted that numeration is a relatively young art. There are still nations that cannot count three. But, what says more than anything, language diminishes the farther we look back, in such a way that we cannot forbear concluding it must once have had no existence at all. Here I am touching upon the difficult question as to the connection between language and thought; and indeed I can to-day do no more than touch upon it. We can only imagine man to have at any time been without language under the supposition that the other advantage which distinguishes him now, reason, had not as yet manifested itself either. In the case of certain ideas, the dependence on the words is more particularly obvious. Thus the numbers, for instance, cannot possibly be separated from the numerals. Mere sight scarcely shows the difference between nine and ten. A child that cannot count will not perceive that of ten cherries one or two have secretly been taken away. For larger numbers counting is absolutely requisite; without it no one will be able to distinguish a hundred objects or persons from ninety-nine. The dim feeling of the more or less which here supplies the place of consciousness would, if we wholly lacked names for the qualities, resemble the not less vague feeling that the one differed from the other, but we should not be able to account for it. Where language does not suffice, we are to this day in the same position. We cannot, for instance, clearly explain to ourselves wherein the difference between the national features of Frenchmen and Germans consists. Let us imagine a time when as yet there was no definite designation for *black*, and the contrast

between the negro and the white man will be found
to have then been doubtless perceived equally vaguely.
If now, again, there was a time when man had no such
words as " lamb," " dog," or " cat," the perception of the
differences between these species of animals must have
been much less distinct than ours. Though a dog
differs considerably enough from a cat, and though we
all alike think of something definite in using the word
" dog," yet it will be extremely difficult to an individual
not scientifically trained to state at once the characteristics by which a dog may be at a glance distinguished from a cat. He will, if he tries, soon perceive
that he never thought of the minute differences, but
had always contented himself with the vague impression which all the characteristics taken together produce. And it is just here where the origin of the word
played a great part. We must consider what a great
difference in the understanding of a piece of music the
knowledge of the notes makes; how the non-profes-
sional man in a changed melody notices indeed the
change, but only obscurely and without knowing in
what it consists. But notes are to music what language is to the objects of human thought.

Now, if the mind of man, according to all this,
exhibits at that dark, immeasurably distant period,
when language had not yet originated, an immense
inferiority to its present condition, we shall in the
next instance be eager to learn wherein his actual
divergence from the animal consisted. And this eagerness will be the greater, as in this very divergence

the reason will have to be found why he in the sequel
developed language and reason and the animal did not.
This question, I think, can only be answered out of
language and its earliest contents themselves.   I believe I have found out that language originally and
essentially expressed only visible activities.   And this
circumstance remarkably coincides with the fact that
animals, especially mammalia, have   only   a   very
limited   sense   for   the   visible   world   in   itself.   On
the   whole,   it   is   true,   they   see   the   same   that   we
do,   but   they   take   interest   in   but   few   things.   The
dog, *e.g.*, recognises his food solely by scent, so that
when his olfactory nerve is cut through   he is quite
at   a   loss   how   to   choose   his   nourishment, and com-
mits the most incredible mistakes.   When the traveller
Kohl traversed the steppes of South Russia, the well-
known phenomenon of the Fata Morgana appeared on
the horizon, and raised within him, as if by enchant-
ment, the illusory hope of finding in the arid, waterless
plains a large refreshing surface of water.   His Tartar
coachman explained the phenomenon, adding the horses
could not be deceived, "for," said he, "they smell the
water."   The same may be said of the camels of the
Arabian desert: they, too, are not exposed to the dis-
appointments which occasionally await the languishing
caravan through the flattering sense of sight.   Certainly
there are individual objects which interest the eyes
of the mammalia, especially of the carnivorous species.
At least I have decidedly noticed a cat being deeply
interested in pigeons flying past at a rather considerable

distance, though she could see them only through a closed window. Of course, it was only a very selfish interest that actuated her.

It is only in the ape that the sense of sight and the interest in the visible world assumes more importance. We see mankind at a low stage of civilisation still availing themselves of the faculty of scent, and examining objects by its means, while we are wholly deficient in such a faculty. At length sight attains higher and higher dominion, and the interest concentrated upon it seems therefore to be the real privilege of man. If now it could be proved that the importance of sight increased and extended in the course of history such as it is reflected in language, such a fact would be tantamount to a development of our race from a mere animal to a human nature. And it does seem capable of proof. Reason in the species at large undergoes the same process as that which in individual instances we witness in ourselves on a smaller scale. When the Romans for the first time came into contact with the Germans, they were so overwhelmingly struck by their high statures, blue defiant eyes, and light hair, that Tacitus says they all look alike. We should at first receive the same impression among a negro population. A nearer acquaintance enables us to perceive the differences which previously escaped us. Something analogous happened to the earliest generations of man, only that it was the whole of creation which they had first slowly to learn partly to distinguish according to its individual objects and partly to notice at least with interest. And what may it have been which they soonest noticed in such a way? It was that which was nearest their hearts—the motions and actions of their fellow-men. For what ever again captivates and gratifies man most is man. Even the glory of Nature herself would fill us with shuddering if we knew ourselves alone, quite alone. Only exceptionally and temporarily things that do not live and act as we do can affect us. I will not attempt to describe the moment when for the first time the impression of a human motion found sympathetic expression in an uttered sound. But permit me to mention an incident which I have myself witnessed, not without surprise, and which is analogous to the moment that lies at such an immeasurable distance beyond all our recollection. A boy who had been almost totally bereft of hearing by an illness at an age when he was already able to lisp a child's first words, passed with his mother through our town on her way to our vicinity, where she hoped to get her unhappy child cured. The handsome, lively boy was then six years old, and had long since forgotten the little he had ever spoken. He had lost all power of speech, but he could hear loud, rumbling noises. A carriage happened to drive past, unseen by him. Quite like a younger child that can hear, the boy put his finger to his ear, prepared to listen, and then waved his hand as if he were cracking a whip. It was, therefore, not the rolling of the wheels which he heard, nor the trotting of the horses which had most vividly impressed him. He chose, out of all that belonged to the carriage, only the one human action which he had witnessed on beholding the phenomenon of the rolling carriage, and imitated that action. And he did so in order to communicate his impression; but the whole interest of this communication consisted for the child only in the desire of awakening the like sensation within us that he felt; it was, in fact, only an expression of his own inward sensation. And such an expression, without any other purpose but the impulse to express ourselves, to give utterance to our joyful interest in what we see, we must assume to have alone originated the first sound, the germ of all speech.

The evolution of language, which has long since clothed with its sounds the whole rich intellectual world from one primitive sound, has perhaps at first sight something surprising in it; but there is no other solution of the riddle involved in it. The various attempts to find a reason why we name one object by one sound, another by another, have failed. We can, indeed, find a reason why we designate the head of man by the word *Kopf.* This word is nearly related to *Kufe* (coop or vat). *Kopf,* properly speaking, means skull, and in all probability in the sense of a drinking vessel, reminding us of those days when the skull of the enemy was converted into a drinking-cup. We likewise know "foot" to be derived from a root implying "to tread." But as we proceed the possibility of assigning reasons ceases. The root of "foot," just mentioned, was primarily *pad;* but why the sound *pad*

happened to be chosen for the meaning of " to tread "
cannot be accounted for. It was thought, down to
the most recent date, that the oldest roots had been
imitations of animal sounds; others have seen in them
a kind of interjection, such as ah! eh! In the one
case the root *pad* would be an imitation of the sounds
produced by steps; in the other, perhaps an expression
of the surprise that was felt on hearing such steps.
Max Müller has sneered at both these hypotheses,
bestowing on them the appellation of bow-wow and
pah-pah theories — bow-wow being intended for an
onomatopœtic designation of the dog. He himself is
of opinion that man is a sounding being; that his soul,
in the earliest times, by means of a now lost faculty,
like a metal, as it were, had responded to the ring of
various objects in nature, and thus produced words.
This view has not escaped a sneer on its part either.
It has in England been called the ding-dong theory.
What alone perfectly corresponds with experience is,
that from one word several others spring differing in
sound and meaning. A word for shell (*Schale*) may, on
the one hand, come to mean husk, and on the other be
used for tortoise-shell, drinking-cup, nay, for head.

But that in this way all words have proceeded from
one original form has not only its significant analogy
in the history of the evolution of the organisms in the
animal and vegetable kingdoms, but also in the origin
of the nations, such as language itself teaches it. How
different are Germans and Hindoos! How much does
the German language differ from the Sanskrit! Only

science recognises their identity, and shows that what is now different must once have been identical. And if we compare the difference between French and Italian with the much greater one between German and Sanskrit, and consider that only the longer separation and greater distance of the nations from each other has called forth these differences, we shall at least not deem it impossible that all the languages of the earth have sprung from one single germ, and have only grown to be so very different by a still longer period of separation. That variety should proceed from unity seems to be the great fundamental law of all evolution, both physical and mental. In language this law leads us back to a quite insignificant germ, a first sound which expressed the excessively little, the only thing that man then noticed and saw with interest; and from that germ the whole wealth of language—aye, I do not hesitate to pronounce it as my conviction—all languages were gradually developed in the course of many, very many millennia.

Thus we have come down to a primitive condition of man's mind, of which both the prospect and retrospect is equally great, far-reaching, marvellous, aye, even deeply affecting. The moment when the faculty of speech took its rise cannot well have coincided with that of his coming into being. As a being that neither speaks nor thinks, at least certainly not in the sense in which we are conscious of thinking as our own inborn human possession, man belongs to another sphere, and becomes subject to the history of the evolution of the animal

kingdom. Thanks to the aid of language, the fortunes of humanity, from its emerging from the animal
condition up to its complete maturity, lie spread out
more clearly before us. These I have to-day endeavoured cursorily to pass in review before you. It could
not be my intention to convince by proofs, seeing that
in such a narrow compass they would probably have
been mere semblances of proofs. Enough for me if I
have succeeded in awakening within you a sense of the
mighty past of the human race. Of such unfathomable
depth nature is here too! Our deeds, our thoughts, all
have an incalculably old pedigree, and to be man is a
high nobility, though one that is newly acquired by
taking a higher flight from generation to generation.

No doubt occasionally, when on the farthest horizon
the infancy of our race is seen to rise, when of the
noble features which confer on man's stature its proud
dignity, one after another threatens to fade from his
picture, a melancholy, an uneasiness may seize us on
looking down from the height on which we stand to so
low a depth, in fact, on our primeval, now so metamor-
phosed, selves. But between the infancy of man and his
manhood lie the well-preserved ideals of his youth, the
virgin blossoms of his thoughts, his works of art, religion, and morality, the offspring of his beautiful and
glowing inspiration. The veneration for the lofty creations of antiquity, the admiration of all the great things
that preceded us, and that we now, combined as they
are to such wealth, are permitted to behold, enjoy, and
understand—these are our own undiminished posses-

sions, inviolable like an imperishable sanctuary. And who would venture to assert that we have already reached the goal? Who knows whether the mighty movement which now, seizing all the nations of the earth, its waves rolling farther and farther, and rising higher and higher, and uncontrollably transforming our feeling, thinking, and acting, is not that very everlastingly young impulse of growth and development? And should there still be on this dark path on which we are led, without man's own individual will being able materially to promote or check his progress, any guiding star, any ray of enlightenment, it will probably be nought else but that very light of consciousness which is dawning upon us in our days—the consciousness of our past.

II.

The Earliest History of the Human Race in the Light of Language, with Special Reference to the Origin of Tools.

[Read before the International Congress for Archæology and History at Bonn, September 15, 1868.]

THE questions which have been placed at the head of your transactions comprise subjects of mighty import to the history of man, and, at the same time, of an almost unlimited range. If I now venture to express my views on a part of them, I am aware that the shortness of the time allotted to me will permit me to place only a very slight sketch before you, and I have asked permission to speak less for the purpose of discussing results than with a view to directing your attention to an important source and method for such inquiries, hitherto taken notice of but sparingly. Archæology proper, *i.e.*, the searching out and investigating of palpable relics of antiquity, has to contend with difficulties which, it would seem, menace to set it limits before it can reach its final goal. I will say nothing about the more accidental difficulty of determining with certainty, in each instance, the age of an object found, and of duly appropriating it. But the higher the antiquity and the more primitive the condition of man, the more imperfect and the less durable must be his works, at least beyond a certain boundary: thus fewer relics will obviously have been preserved of a wood age than of a stone or metal age. At the same time, too, man's works are always the less recognisable the less artistic they are. We might, therefore, just happen to discover, from times which are the most important to the origin of things, implements in which we could not with certainty recognise the human hand that fashioned them. Besides, it is with these rude productions of art as with everything that has come into being; we see them lie before us, indeed, but they tell us nothing about their origin or the mental process that preceded it. If there ever was a time when man was as yet without any tools and altogether without any industrial art, his earliest dwellings can at most manifest this to us by silence. Precisely as regards that remote period, I believe I may appeal to language as a living testimony, and I would beg of you to permit me just to touch upon this linguistic archæology, the results of which I hope soon to publish in the second volume of my work on the Origin of Language and Reason.

Man had language before he had tools, and before he practised industrial arts. This is a proposition which, obvious and probable in itself, also admits of complete proof from language. On considering a word denoting an activity carried on with a tool, we shall invariably find it not to have been its original meaning, but that it previously implied a similar activity requiring only the natural organs of man. Let us, *e.g.*, compare the ancient word *mahlen* (to grind), *Mühle* (mill), Latin, *molo*, Greek, μύλη. The process, well known from antiquity, of grinding the grains of the bread-fruit between stones, is no doubt simple enough to be pre-supposed as practised already in the primitive period in one form or another. Nevertheless, the word that we now use for an activity with implements has pro-ceeded from a still more simple conception. The root *mal* or *mar*, so widely diffused in the Indo-European family of languages, implies "to grind with the fingers" as well as "to crush with the teeth." I would remind you of *mordeo*, "to bite," and the Sanskrit root *mrid*, which implies to pulverise and to rub, *e.g.*, one's forehead with one's hand; of the Greek μολύνω, to spread over and soil with flour, mud, or the like, which may be compared to the Sanskrit *mala*, "soiling," Gothic *mulda*, "soft earth." On the one hand, μέλας, "black," on the other, μαλακός, *mollis*, "mellow," belong to this class; aye, so do even a number of designations of morass-like fluids and the word *Meer* (sea). In German, two different words from cognate roots per-fectly coincide in sound: the *mahlen* (grinding) of the corn and the *malen* (painting) of pictures. The fundamental meaning of both is to rub or spread with the fingers; and an equally close resemblance may be found in the designation of these two notions in the Latin *pinso* and *pingo*.

This phenomenon of the activity with implements deriving its name from one more simple, ancient, and brute-like, is quite universal; and I do not know how otherwise to account for it but that the name is older than the activity with tools which it denotes at the present time; that, in fact, the word was already extant before men used any other organs but the native and natural ones. Whence does sculpture derive its name? *Sculpo* is a collateral form of *scalpo*, and at first implied only scratching with nails. The art of weaving or matting is of primeval date; it plays a part in the earliest religious myths. History records no stage of culture which was wholly without it. As the Greeks often describe Athena to be employed in weaving, so do the Veda hymns make the sun-god, the goddess Aramati, and, in a mystic sense, the priests, occupy themselves with that work. Of the sun-god, *e.g.*, they say, with reference to the alternation of day and night, " Such is the divinity of Surya, such his greatness, that amid his work he draws in again the stretched-out web." The root here used for to stretch out at the same time supplies the word for the warp of the texture, while the weft in Sanskrit is denoted by the root *ve*, the simpler form of our word *wcben* (to weave), similar to the English weft and woof. If, now, we compare with this root the various others closely related to it, and beginning with the same consonant (*w*), *e.g.*, the Latin *vieo*, many of them afford a hint enabling us to say on which objects the art of weaving, or rather matting, may first have been employed. The

Latin *vimen*, for instance, which, properly speaking, implies a means for matting, is used of branches of trees and shrubs in their natural state and growth, and especially so far as they are worked up into all kinds of wickerwork, or serve as ropes for binding, of their artificial state. The *Weide* (willow) derived its name in the earliest times from the special fitness of its branches for such purposes, and so did many species of grass and reeds. That plant the fibres of which have pre-eminently continued among us to be made use of in the art of weaving, viz., *Flachs* (flax), has its name from *flechten* (plaiting), as *Flechse* (tendon), *i.e.*, "band, sinew," clearly shows.

Simple mattings of fibres of plants and of flexible twigs are the first objects of art in this department; but language leads us still a step farther back. There are words in which the idea of the entanglement of the boughs of the bush or of trees with dense foliage is found so intimately allied with the plaiting of plants that it becomes probable this natural plaiting may have served the artistic activity of man as a model. The sight of closely entwined branches and of reeds growing in luxuriant entanglement, keeping pace with the transformation in the culture of man, gradually led to the first roughly plaited mat as a product of his art. Aye, the natural plaiting of the tree was, perhaps, the first object on which his art was practised. There are still extant transitions which render it extremely probable that a kind of nest-building in the branches of trees with dense foliage was natural to

man in the earliest times, and sufficed him for the
preparation of his dwelling. From Africa, in so many
respects a land of wonders as regards the history of
man, the traveller Barth gives an account of the Ding-
Ding people, of whom he says they partly dwell in
trees. In much the same low condition are the extremely barbarous inhabitants of the island of Anna-
tom, who use the branches of certain groups of trees
fit for the purpose as a kind of very primitive hut.
Of the Puris, Prince Maximilian, in his description of
his Brazilian tour, tells us something similar, only that
they, in addition, have the hammock, which is peculiar
to the South Americans, and seems to be a remnant
of their former habit of sleeping between the branches
of trees. The word *Hängematte* (hammock) has come
to us, along with the thing itself, from those parts. It
belongs to the language of Hayti, where Columbus
found it in the form of *amaca*, and whence, in various
languages of Europe, it was transformed into hamac,
hammock, and (among the Dutch) into hangmack, until
finally, by misconception, it became hangmat, *Hänge-*
or *Hänge-matte* (in German).

Another point, viz., the figure of man, seems to me
to be a decided indication that the tree must have been
his original habitation. His erect. gait finds its most
natural explanation in his former climbing mode of life,
and from his habit of clasping the tree in his ascent
we can best explain the transformation of the hand
from a motory organ into a grasping one, so that we
shall be found to owe to the lowest stage of our culture

that seems credible our distinguishing advantages—the free and commanding elevation of our head and the possession of that organ which Aristotle has called the tool of tools.

However mighty the transformation of human activity which the secrets hidden in words betray to us, yet we have no reason for seeing aught else in it but the sum of quite gradual processes, such as, in other instances, we still daily see going on. Since a comparatively few years we have denoted by the word *nähen* (to sew), no longer merely a manual work, but also one of the machine; by *schiessen* (to shoot) we understand something very different from that which was understood by it previously to the invention of gunpowder. How very differently is a ship now constructed from what it was at the time when it differed in nothing from a trough, a hollow wooden vessel, such as the name indicates! How little resemblance is there between our locomotives and the first thing which was called waggon, and which, I have reason to believe, was nothing but a simple stump of a tree rolling downwards! The transformation of man's mode of life proceeds very gradually, and we have the right to assume, I think, that it has never done otherwise. We must guard against ascribing to reflection too large a share in the origin of tools. The first simplest tools were doubtless of incidental origin, like so many other great inventions of modern times. They were probably rather stumbled upon than invented. I have formed this view more particularly from having observed that tools are never named from the process by which they were made, never genetically, but always from the work they are intended for. A pair of shears, a saw, a hoe, are things that shear, saw, or hoe. This linguistic law must appear the more surprising as the implements which are not tools are wont to be designated genetically, or passively, as it were, according to the material of which they are made or the work that produced them. *Schlauch* (hose), *e.g.*, is everywhere thought of as the skin stripped off an animal. Beside the German word *Schlauch* stands the English *slough;* the Greek ἀσκός signifies both hose and skin of an animal. Here, then, language quite plainly teaches us how and of what material the implement called hose was made. With tools such is not the case, and they may, therefore, as far as language is concerned, not have at first been made at all; the first knife may have been a sharp stone accidentally found, and, I might say, employed as if in play.

It might next be imagined that if tools have been named from the work for which they are intended, an idea of such work must have preceded the name ; *e.g.*, if a cutting tool is designated as something cutting, the idea of cutting seems thereby to be presupposed. But we know that all these words originally denoted activities which were carried on without any other than the natural tools. The word "shears" plainly shows this. It denotes at present a double knife, a two-armed cutting tool. I need hardly mention that this meaning was not the original one. Indeed the Hindoos and the

Greeks have a cognate word signifying shearing (or shaving) knife, and the Swedish *skära* means sickle. It may be fairly assumed that shears and shearing knives were primarily used by the Indo-European nomads of primitive times in shearing sheep. At the same time, however, the custom, not of shearing sheep, but of plucking them with the hand, may be traced down to comparatively late times. Varro maintains it to have been the general process previous to the invention of the shears, but he also speaks of such as were still practising it in his days; and even Pliny says, "Sheep are not shorn everywhere; in some places the custom of plucking continues" (viii. 2, 73). The close connection between the word *scheren* (to shear) and *scharren* (to scrape), and, among others too, the Old High German name of the mole, *scëro*, the scraping animal, render it besides more than probable that again the original meaning of the word was only to shave, to scratch, to scrape, and show the shears there-fore to have been conceived as a tool for scraping and scratching the skin for the purpose of plucking it. In this way we may suppose the names of the tools and the work done with them sprung by a slow process from a quite gradual evolution of human movements, such as they were already from the first possible to the body of man left to itself.

Permit me, gentlemen, on this occasion, at least to point out a most important difference, which is cal-culated to make the expression "evolution" as applied to the tool a full truth. I mean the difference between primary and secondary tools. The tool, observed in its evolution, marvellously resembles a natural organ; exactly like this it has its transformations and its differentiations. We should wholly misconceive the tool if we always wanted to find the cause of its origin in its immediate purpose, just as we should misconceive the webbed foot of the duck were we to think of it as unconnected with the formation of the feet of birds that cannot swim. Thus, *e.g.*, Klemm has already drawn attention to the fact that the gimlet originated in the fire-drill of primitive times, that remarkable apparatus, the common use of which in various parts of the earth quite remote from each other would alone suffice to let us presume an external connection, an intercommunication between the various peoples of the earth to an almost unbounded extent. The aborigines of North and South America, from the Aleutes to the Pescheræ, and the Caffres in South Africa, as well as the Australians, have the custom of drilling a stick of hard wood into a softer one, and to turn it round in the latter until the shavings themselves and the dry leaves used as tinder ignite. It is well known that this process, which, as contrasted with the use of the flint, represents the wood age, is met with in quite a surprising agreement in the Veda hymns, where the two *arani* or friction-sticks play an important part in the sacrifice. Nor is this a solitary instance in which archæology and linguistics teach us to trace back the condition of highly civilised nations to the lowest stage of culture still to be met with among one or the other savage

tribe, and lets us recognise a *universal law* where we at
first should have been disposed to see an isolated pecu-
liarity. There is hidden in the history of language,
nay in what often even later writers of antiquity betray
to us, an immense deal which is of importance to the
knowledge of our earliest history, and it will be pains
well bestowed to penetrate into these depths and dig
up their treasures.

An analogy to the origin of the secondary tool by
transformation is presented by the development of the
musical string from the bowstring, such as Wilkinson
has pointed it out. How well the bowstring was cal-
culated to excite the musical sense to such an application is shown in a remarkable passage in Homer:
"As when a man skilled on the cithern and in song
lightly fastens the string to a new peg, tightening
on both sides the well-twisted sheep-gut, so without
labour Odysseus stretched his great bow. Then with
his right hand he seized the string and examined it;
it emitted a beautiful sound, resembling the voice of a
swallow" (Odyss. 21, 406 *sqq.*). How comparatively recent stringed instruments are may be inferred from the
circumstance alone that, at the time of the discovery of
America by the Europeans, none such were met with
among the indigenous population. If we consider of
what importance the sight of the vibrating string is to
musical consciousness, we must admire the momentous
effects which were produced by a trifling and accidental
observation, by the chance possession of a bow provided
with a vibrating sinew.

In order to recognise how much we are ourselves
still undergoing the process of a like transformation,
and to gain, at the same time, a standard by which to
judge of those [remote] processes, it suffices to point
out the quite modern invention of the umbrella, which
is an imitation of the primitive parasol, only for
a different purpose.   The parachute of aeronauts is
likewise such a transformation.   Do not such developments of the productions of man's ideas and volition
present a parallel to what happens in nature when,
under altered conditions and necessities, the arm is, in
the case of birds, converted into a wing?   But it may
here be mentioned that the parasol, in the earliest
times, served religious purposes, and we here arrive at
a new point of the highest moment in the history of
implements, which I can here only touch upon.   Religion, in its primitive form, gives so mighty an impulse
to the customs, conceptions, and creations of man—it
was, in fact, the source of so much of whose connection with religion we have not the faintest notion—that
without entering upon its investigation we are unable
ever to learn to understand from an historical point of
view our own doings, and more especially the objects
that surround us, that have been produced by our hand,
and distinguish us in our outward life from the brute.

The use of implements shaped by himself is more
decidedly than aught else an evident distinctive char-
acteristic of man's mode of life.   For this reason the
question as to the origin of the tool is a subject of the
greatest moment in our early history, and I therefore

thought I might treat the question as to the nature of the implements of man in primitive times in this partly rather narrower, partly wider sense. I do not hesitate to assert that there must have been a time when man did not possess any implements or tools, but contented himself to work wholly with his natural organs; that then followed a period when he was already able to recognise and use accidentally found objects resembling those organs, and by their aid to enlarge, heighten, and arm the power of his natural tools; *e.g.*, to employ a hollow shell of a plant as a substitute for the hollow hand, which was the first vessel. Not until after the employment of these objects that accidentally presented themselves had become familiar did man's creative activity in the shape of imitation take its rise.

[Perhaps, gentlemen, you will the more readily permit me to cast a side glance at one special preparative activity, seeing that it is likewise connected with another subject proposed to this meeting for discussion, viz., our nourishment. Among the various modes of preparing food, boiling is naturally one of the most recent. Cook found the aborigines of Tahiti totally unacquainted with the process of boiling in pots; meat they roasted either by the fire or in earth-holes between hot stones. The Homeric heroes, too, ate their meat roasted on the spit or stewed in the pan; boiling it in water seems to have been unknown to the poet. Thus, too, the German word *kochen*, "to boil," is a foreign word derived from the Latin *coquo*.

The idea is clearly developed from direct preparations
by the fire, such as roasting and baking, even in
words from which these meanings were subsequently
wholly excluded. One more step and we find these
very words, which, from denoting the effect of the
boiling water, have returned to express that of the
fire, used of the sun. Thus the Greek πέσσω, "to
cook," still implies in Homer to ripen, and this meaning the Sanskrit *pak* likewise bears. The Russian
petch still signifies the burning, stinging of the sun.
A very remarkable adjective from the same root, in
its notional relations common to the early period of
the Greek and Sanskrit languages, leads us still farther.
It is the Greek πέπων, Sanskrit *pъkva*. Πέπων, signifies "ripe;" in Homer and Hesiod, however, it does
not occur in this sense, but in another which cannot
have sprung from the former. They invariably use
it as an address; in two passages it signifies a reproach
for indolence or cowardice; in many others, however,
it is equivalent to "O dear one." In observing the
use of the word *pakva* in the Veda hymns we shall
not be able to find in it a reference to cooking or
ripening either; it there obviously means only "sweet"
or "eatable." The fact is, it is used not only of grain,
of a tree, of branches, when it may mean to ripen,
but also of milk in the frequently recurring thought
"In the living cows, the black, the red, thou hast
put the milk, ready and white." "Sweet" may be the
meaning of the Greek word too in the insinuating
address, and when, *e.g.*, the dazzled Cyclop in the

"Odyssey" says to his favourite ram, κριὲ πέπον, we shall have to render it by "sweet or tender ram." As a reproach, however, it would, according to the development of the word, mean effeminate or lazy. Herewith, then, all that refers to the preparation of food has disappeared from the word *kochen* (to cook), for to this the adjective in question bears close affinity. From something soft and eatable, let us say, from some fruit met with in this condition, the idea merges into that of softening by the sun, by fire, or boiling water. By the way, let me observe here that language shows no period when man did not eat meat; on the contrary, it seems to have been his earliest food. At the same time there is nothing to show that it was from the first prepared in any way; it was, doubtless, for a long time consumed in a raw state only.]

The vestiges of his earliest conceptions still preserved in language proclaim it loudly and distinctly that man has developed from a state in which he had solely to rely on the aid of his organs, differed little in his habits from the brute creation, and with respect to the enjoyment of existence, nay, to his preservation, depended almost entirely on whatever lucky chance presented to him. He became more powerful the more his ability to avail himself of the things around him increased. And how came it to be increased? Simply because his *faculty of perceiving the things* increased, a faculty which is none other than reason itself. It is the theoretical nature of man

that has made him so great. The present age has
opened for the tool a new grand development; it
creates in the machine, which is constantly being
perfected and becomes more and more powerful, an
implement emancipated from the hand of man, and
inspiring its own maker with a peculiar admiration.
It is not accidental that in this same age mankind
should endeavour with so much consciousness to
reflect on its past, and a meeting such as yours should
make the beginnings of human culture the subject
of its scientific investigations and debates. The state
of culture of our species and its historical consciousness are quantities that increase simultaneously. We
at once, with wistful and searching glances, take a
retrospective view of the dark past from which we
have started, and with bold hope look forward towards
the no less dark goal whither we are being led. Shall
we ever wholly penetrate the night of the primeval
ages? Shall we ever reach the goal of perfection
that so temptingly lures us onward from afar? We
do not know. But our inner impulse irresistibly urges
us on to pursue our inquiries in either direction and
bids us march on!

III.

On Colour-Sense in Primitive Times and its Development.

[Read before the Meeting of German Naturalists at Frankfcrt-on-the-Maine, September 24, 1867.]

THE subject to which, for a brief space, I would request your attention, will, I hope, not be found unworthy of it. Has human sensation, has perception by the senses, a history? Were the organs of man's senses thousands of years ago in the same condition as now, or can we perhaps prove that at some remote period these organs must have been incapable of some of their present functions? These questions, it is true, fall within the province of physiology, or, if I am permitted to coin the term, of *palæo-physiology ;* but the means of answering them necessarily differ to some extent from those which in general are at the command of natural science. By means of geological "finds" we may gain a conception of the skeleton, and perhaps the whole external appearance, of an extinct species of animals; we can from remnants of skulls draw general conclusions as to an imperfectly developed human race of early times; but it would be difficult to form an idea from the sight of the head, the remnants of which have been preserved in the Neander valley as a problem for our days, as to how it may have thought. Fortunately, the history of the mind, too, has its primeval relics, its deposits and petrifactions of another kind, affording more instructive explanations than one should be inclined to believe; and, if carefully pursued, they lead to perhaps unexpected, but, I think, on that account not less trustworthy results.

The history of colour-sense is of paramount importance to the total development of sensation. In the earliest mental productions that are preserved to us of the various peoples of the earth there lies stored up an uncommonly rich material for the study of the impression which colour made in primitive times; and I beg, in the first instance, to direct your attention to a negative result that arises from a search into that rich material. At an early stage, notwithstanding a thousand obvious and often urgently pressing occasions that presented themselves, the *colour blue* is not mentioned at all. If we consider the nature of the books to which this observation applies, the idea of chance must here be excluded. Let me first mention the wonderful, youthfully fresh hymns of the Rigveda, the discovery of which amidst the mass of Indian literature seems destined to become as important to the present century in awakening a sense of genuine antiquity as the revival of Greek antiquity at the threshold of modern times was to that period in

D

arousing the sense of beauty and artistic taste. These hymns, consisting of more than 10,000 lines, are nearly all filled with descriptions of the sky. Scarcely any other subject is more frequently mentioned; the variety of hues which the sun and dawn daily display in it, day and night, clouds and lightnings, the atmosphere and the ether, all these are with inexhaustible abundance exhibited to us again and again in all their magnificence; only the fact that the sky is blue could never have been gathered from these poems by any one who did not already know it himself. I refrain from adducing proofs, which, in order to be exhaustive, might easily swell on to the entire contents of the books, and will only state, with respect to the astronomical standpoint of those poems, that, according to all appearance, they know of a lunar year with a thirteenth intercalary month; in genuine passages, however, hardly the name of any constellation is mentioned, and most certainly not the difference between planets and fixed stars, which, indeed, belongs to the relatively late discoveries of the ancient science of astronomy.

The Veda hymns represent the earliest stage of the human mind that has been preserved in any literature, if one may use this term of hymns transmitted orally. But as regards the blue colour, the same observation may be made of the *Zendavesta*, the books of the Parsees, to whom, as is well known, light and fire, both the terrestrial and heavenly, are most sacred, and of whom one may expect an attention to the thousand-fold hues of the sky similar to that in the Vedas. The *Bible*, in which, as is equally well known, the sky or heaven plays no less a part, seeing that it occurs in the very first verse, and in upwards of 430 other passages besides, quite apart from synonymous expressions, such as ether, &c., yet finds no opportunity either of mentioning the blue colour. Nay, even in the *Homeric Poems* the blue sky is not mentioned, although in the regions where they originated, it exercises such a special charm on every visitor.

You will grant that such a series of agreements cannot well be deemed mere chance, but that we must seek an explanation of them in some law.

The words by which we designate the colours are divided in two easily recognised classes. The most definite, but at the same time most recent terms, are as a rule derived from objects which have a definite hue and admit of easy comparison, *e.g.*, *strohgelb* (straw-yellow), *veilchenblau* (violet-blue), *rosa* (pink). Such terms are artificial. At the time when words originated naturally, people contented themselves with the contrast, for instance, between the yellow and the red; all particulars appeared as insignificant niceties. In all spheres in which we are able to separate in language more recent notions from older ones we observe something analogous. The notions start from extremities, and gradually pass on to designations of similar things of a less extreme character. I can here state this law only thus broadly. As to the colours, the indifference with respect to the intermediate ones rises, as we ap-

proach primeval ages, to an ever-increasing degree, until
at length only the outermost extremes, black and red,
are left.   Aye, the historical progress may be shown to
have taken place in conformity with the *scheme of the
colour-spectrum*, so that, *e.g.*, the sensibility to yellow
was awakened before that to green.   On the other hand,
language, as may be easily conceived, does not acknowledge the proposition that black is no colour ; it desig-
nates it at a very early period as the most decided
contrast to red ; nay, more, it joins the weakest tone of
the colour-scale for which it has still a name, viz., blue,
to this dark end.

Of the words that in any language are used for *blue*,
a smaller number originally signified *green ;* the greater
number in the earliest time signified *black*.   This applies to our term *blau* (blue), which is to be met with in
the Old North in the compound *blá-madhr*, " black man,
Moor," and is related to the English " black."   It equally
applies, to mention a remote example, to the Chinese
hiuan, which at present signifies *sky-blue*, but in early
times meant *black*.   In ancient books it occurs in the
combination *hiuan te*, *te* meaning virtue or merit, and
both words together naturally not blue, but obscure or
unknown merit.   A word for blue at present diffused
over a great part of Asia is *nil*, probably identical with
the name of the Nile, which seems to be derived from
the Persians.[1]   *Nîla*, too, in ancient writings, signifies

[1] The Nile, according to Greek records, is said to have originally
been called "the Black."   The name Neilos does not occur as yet in
Homer (the Nile with him is called Aigyptos), and in Hesiod is perhaps not to be understood as applying to the Egyptian, but to some
mythological river.

only black, and is nothing but the Hindoo form of the Latin *niger*.

What may have been the physiological condition of a generation that could have called the colour of the sky only black? Does the contrast with us consist in the appellation or in the perception? In this respect it is interesting to notice the singular gravity with which different colours bearing one name are considered alike. Thus a Hindoo philosopher, in investigating the cause of the blue colour of the sky, quotes a certainly somewhat strange opinion, according to which the cause is subjective, and the black colour of the eye is communicated to the heavens, just as to the jaundiced eye everything looks yellow.

No one, I should think, who reflects on the way in which Homer speaks of blue and violet objects will fail to be somewhat surprised. According to the analogies already cited, it may be less surprising that the word κύανος, our *Cyan*, is with him the deepest black. The mourning garment of Thetis he calls κυάνεον, and at the same time "black as no other garment." The same colour-term is applied to the storm-cloud and the black cloud of death, and several times, by adding μέλας, it is distinctly explained as black. On the contrary, Odysseus' hair is likened to the hyacinth, and the ancient Greek commentators, to whom the conception was not yet so foreign as to us, quite correctly refer the simile to the black colour. Pindar speaks in the same sense of violet locks, and Homer of iron as of violet hue. When Mr. Gladstone, while at the head of the adminis-

tration of the Ionic Islands, devoted his leisure to
Homeric studies, he did not fail to perceive how surprising such and similar passages were, and he was
thereby tempted to give credit to the ancient legend
according to which Homer is said to have shared the
lot which he himself ascribes to a bard of the prehistoric
world: "The Muse bestowed on him good and evil;
she bereft him of his sight and gave him sweet songs."
If, however, this pathological explanation should apply
to Homer (his individual existence presupposed), many
other poets of antiquity, the whole human race itself,
must have been in the same condition during a whole
series of millennia. Only the Egyptians form a partial exception here; but who indeed would quote the
builders of the giant-temple of Karnak as a proof with
respect to primeval times ? On the other hand, it is
noteworthy down to what a late period both the Greeks
and the Romans still confounded blue and violet, especially with grey and brown. Even long after scientific
observation had separated these colours they seem to
have been mixed up together in popular conception.
And thus it happened that Theocritus, and, in imitation of him, Virgil, by way of excuse for the bronzed
hue of a beautiful face, could still say, "Are not the
violets, too, and the hyacinths black ?" With a similar
intention Virgil says : "The white privets fall; it is the
black hyacinths which are sought after and loved."
Nay, even Cassiodorus, at the beginning of the sixth
century after Christ, gives an account of the four colours
employed in the Circensian games, which, as is well

known, sometimes acquired a fatal significance : green
had been dedicated to spring, red to summer, white,
on account of the hoar-frost, to autumn, blue to the
cloudy winter—*venetus nubilæ hiemi.* Classical antiquity, in fact, possessed no word for pure blue. The
Latin *cœruleus* is of a slipperiness which has at times
driven philologists to despair ; it runs through a development from black passing through grey towards
blue. The Romanic languages found indeed no fit word
for blue in the original Roman tongue, and were obliged
partly to borrow it from the Germans. Thus, among
others, the French *bleu* and the older Italian *biavo* are,
as is well known, borrowed from our *blau,* which, in
its turn, as I have stated before, in the earliest time
signified black.[1]

In a certain respect, it is true, a parallel to this singular fact of a pathological kind seems to present itself.
Goethe mentions two young men, not above twenty years
of age, whose sight in general was keen enough, but in
whom he observed a condition which he calls *Akyano-
blepsy,* and he accounts for it by their having no eye for
blue. He is of opinion that the sky appeared to them
rose colour, and everything green in tones from yellow
to russet, somewhat like what it appears to us in autumn.

---

[1] The *Koran* does not as yet know the blue colour either, however
much it speaks of the heavens. On the other hand, the Arabic philosopher Al-Kindi in the ninth century wrote a treatise " On the Nature
of the Sphere and the constant Azure-like Hue which is observed in the
Direction towards Heaven." Nor is the blue sky mentioned in the
Edda hymns. In the Alvis-hymn, *igroen* (all-green) is enumerated
among the names of the earth, but among the appellations of the sky
enumerated by the side of them none refers to its colour. ,

" If," he says, " one leaves conversation with them to chance, and interrogates them only on objects lying before them, one becomes quite confused and is afraid of going mad. With a little method, however, one may come considerably nearer an understanding of the law of this abnormity." In these words Goethe at once pretty accurately describes what we feel in attempting to determine the real value of the ancient terms for colours. Without venturing actually to draw a comparison between the two conditions,[1] I must nevertheless be allowed to state that the agreement with regard to green appears to me even more striking than that respecting blue.

The *colour green* is met with in antiquity one stage farther back than the blue, then to disappear likewise. Naturally people saw green objects while there was vegetation on earth; and if the heavens from holy causes engaged their attention, the earth, on which they and their cattle fed, could not interest them less. Yet the ten books of Rigveda hymns, though they frequently mention the earth, no more bestow on it the epithet green than on the heavens that of blue. They speak of trees, herbs, and fodder-grass, of ripe branches, lovely fruit, food-yielding mountains, of sowing and ploughing, but never of green fields. Still more surprising is the same phenomenon in the Zendavesta. In that book the interest in the earth and its fertility is still more prominent; the condition of the people resulting from it is founded on agriculture; the

---

[1] Cf. Dr. Brandis's letter on the subject in Goethe's works, vol. xl. p. 49.

tillers of the soil occupy the third rank, by the side of warriors and priests. In an apostrophe to the personified holy sacrificial plant Haoma we read, "I praise the earth, the wide, broad, fertile, patient, that bore thee; I praise the soil where thou didst grow in fragrance." The trees are designated as fruitful, beautiful, shot up, mighty, and, finally, in one passage, too, as golden-hued, with reference to the gold of the fruits. As regards the Greeks, χλωρός, which Hesiod uses of a green bough, in the Homeric poems almost everywhere quite unmistakably signifies yellow: it alternates with ὤχρος, whence our *Ocher* (ochre) is derived. Only in a later hymn to Apollo the same epithet bears the sense of the green of the mountain and the visible impression of the vegetable kingdom, which till then we find taken notice of only from the aspect of its utility, *i.e.*, in so far as it is appreciable by the taste. Yet the Greek word has never wholly acquired the meaning of our *green*, but always only that of a beginning of that colour, including yellow; and so late as in the Aristotelian "Book of Colours" it is contrasted with the proper green, which is paraphrased by "grass-coloured" or "leek-coloured."

Another remarkable instance of the difference in the conception of a natural phenomenon at different periods is the *rainbow*. Aristotle, in his "Meteorology," calls it tri-coloured, viz., red, yellow, and green. Two centuries before, Xenophanes had said, "What they call Iris is likewise a cloud, purple, reddish, and yellow in appearance;" where he leaves out the green, or, at all events, does not clearly define it. In the Edda, too, the rainbow is explained to be a tri-coloured bridge.

Democritus and the Pythagoreans assumed four fundamental colours, *black, white, red,* and *yellow,* a conception which for a long time obtained in antiquity.[1] Nay, ancient writers (Cicero, Pliny, and Quintilian) state it as a positive fact that the Greek painters, down to the time of Alexander, employed only those four colours. This has been deemed incredible, since, with such appliances, neither the green of the earth nor the blue of the sky could be represented. But whatever may be thought of the statement of those writers, judging from the above-mentioned analogies, this objection does not warrant us to pronounce it false. There is nothing at all contradictory in the assumption that those times did not yet feel the want of representing the colours of the heavens and the earth.

In one passage of the Zendavesta we have found the blossoms designated as fragrant; in the Veda hymns I have not met with a similar epithet. The sense of fragrance too—and this remark will perhaps not be found quite unserviceable as an analogy for the questions concerning the sense of sight—has not been at all times innate in man. The custom of offering incense with the sacrifice is not yet met with in the Rigveda, though it is found in the more recent Yadshurveda. Among the biblical books, the sense of the fragrance

---

[1] The Chinese have since olden times assumed five colours, viz., green in addition to the above. The same we meet with among Arabic philosophers.

of flowers first makes its appearance in the " Song of Songs." According to the description in Genesis, there were in Paradise all kinds of trees " that were pleasant to the sight and good for food." The apocryphal book of Henoch (of the last century before Christ, or still somewhat later), extant in Ethiopian, likewise describes Paradise, but does not omit to extol the delightful fragrance of the Tree of Knowledge as well as of other trees of Paradise. That the sense of fragrance is not innate may be proved from language too ; and though it may not be always advisable to draw an exact parallel between the development of the child and that of the human race, yet in this case it is instructive to observe how indifferent children for a long time continue to — fragrance, and even to bad odours. The objection that among the keen senses of savage tribes the sense of smell plays a prominent part is only an apparent one. Scent by means of the sense of smell materially differs, from the sensibility to pleasant or unpleasant sensations that lie in the perception of odour itself ; nay, the two perhaps bear an inverse ratio to each other. As regards the brute creation the fact is self-evident. The dog is distinguished for his scent ; but how much soever this animal is extolled for his good and human-like qualities, his greatest admirer would hardly be tempted to gladden his dog with a nosegay.

The sense of euphony or the pleasure of hearing has a similar history. That sense is not innate in man either. Man does not sing " as the bird sings that lives in the branches." There is no natural song any more than there is any natural plastic art. Art has its laborious reflected development, and with it the sense of art is developed. Here the results of linguistic science meet most decidedly those of physics and physiology.

In returning to the subject of colour-sense, I should like to try and unroll before you, in however concise a completeness, the picture which I have gathered from a thousand details of the literatures and linguistic history of the human race. But I will only detain you some minutes longer in order to add a few words on the range of colours known to the earliest ages. In the genuine ancient Veda hymns there is not only no green, but even their *yellow* is not the pure colour of our spectrum. In the course of centuries the words signifying yellow lapse into the signification of green ; in earlier times they themselves spring from roots by which *gold* is wont to be named, *i.e.*, from *yellow-red* and *red-brown*. When in the pictorial representations in ancient Egyptian tomb-chambers we see the black-red-golden sun-fans carried about, we are reminded of the vast historical background on which is exhibited a primitive type of many a modern object. There really seems to have existed a *black-red-golden age* in the history of the sense of sight. The genuine Rigveda hymns represent this stage in contrast to the white-yellow-red-black of the nascent Greek natural philosophy. In these hymns *white* is scarcely as yet distinguished from *red*.

The circumstance that the colour-terms originate according to a definite succession, and originate so everywhere, must have a common cause. This cause cannot consist in the primarily defective distinction merely, for in the earliest times the colour of the sky is by no means called black or gold-yellow, which would be the proximately fittest word for its designation, but no mention at all is made of it. It would seem, indeed, that we must assume a gradually and regularly rising sensibility to impressions of colour, analogous to that which renders glaring contrasts of colour so unbearable to a cultivated taste, while the uneducated taste loves them. Perhaps, too, the intensity of the original impressions decreases in proportion as their extent and multiplicity increases. To men in the earliest antiquity at least the sense of the colours familiar to them was exceedingly keen and lively. The three phenomena upon which in reality the three colour-notions of that time were based—the night, the dawn, and the sun—produced an impression on the people of those times such as we are now scarcely able to conceive or to feel. The dualism of *black* and *red* stands out in very marked features as a first and most primitive period of all colour-sense behind the one hitherto described. But even this dualistic epoch is not without a recognisable beginning either. We can by the aid of etymology arrive at a still earlier stage, when the notions of black and red coalesce in the vague conception of something coloured.

The final decision as regards the nature of this whole development will only be come to by the co-operation of two scientific disciplines. It will not be possible, without availing ourselves of the important progress and discoveries which have been made in the most recent times precisely in the way of explaining the perception of colour; but neither will it be possible without a regard to the intimate connection of the entire development of language and ideas, and to its bearing on sensation and conception. Here a whole world of antique relics for our investigation lies hidden, not in fragments, but in unbroken, well-connected links. The whole chain of development of each of our ideas up to its most primitive form is lying buried before us in words, and is awaiting its excavation by linguistic science.

I have ventured to appear before you with a view to indicate the results to which this science is capable of leading us. Would I had succeeded in making you, gentlemen, share my own conviction that the time has arrived when linguistic and physical science, conscious of their common aims, must join hands. As the organism, notwithstanding the twofold manifestation of its existence, constitutes an indivisible unity, so only undivided science can lead to a knowledge of it—the science of nature, vast, entire, and indivisible.

P.S.—It is not without some hesitation that I submit the above lecture to the public at large. It could only be a compressed and scanty extract from extensive researches made already ten years ago, and ever since, from time to time, gone into again and completed; so that I am all the more fully aware how much there is still left for competent and reflecting readers to supply

and to object to in its present form. To avoid the
semblance of a completeness which time and place of
delivery forbade me, I have even foreborne to add the
more particular references to the passages quoted. I
hope, however, soon to be able to publish all the facts
bearing upon the questions here mooted, and must entreat
my readers meanwhile to suspend their judgment on
any doubtful point. As regards the general inferences,
too, a fuller examination of many facts stated will
naturally tend to modify them. Since, however, on the
other hand, they likewise partly depend on the decision
as to the relation between ideas and words, notions and
sensations, I beg in this respect to refer to my inquiries
into Language and Reason, of which the first volume is
in the press. What encourages me to do so is the
indulgent and appreciative, and to me highly gratifying,
manner in which the above lecture has been listened to
by an assembly which numbers the most unprejudiced
thinkers and investigators of Germany among its mem-
bers. The universality of German physical science—
a noble acquisition of perhaps only the last decennia—
vouches for its having a great future, which promises to
embrace all the interests of the human race.

IV.

On the Origin of Writing.

[Read before the General Meeting of the German Oriental Society at Würzburg, October 3, 1868.]

IF I undertake to submit for renewed investigation
to a meeting of highly honoured colleagues the question as to the origin of writing, it is not my intention once more here to discuss before you the origin
of alphabetic writing, or of any other fully developed
system. I rather propose to treat here the prehistoric
beginnings of writing, so far as they may be inferred
from the course which their development has taken
since their appearance in history, and from other analogies. Only in this sense I beg you will permit me
to take a brief survey of what has been revealed to
us by historical discoveries about the origin of the
systems of writing at present in use. The alphabets
proper, it is well known, radiate, notwithstanding
all their variety, from but a few centres. We not
only know that our European characters are all primarily of Greek and secondarily of Semitic origin, but
through Professor Mommsen's researches we also know
exactly in what way the Italic alphabets have deve-

loped. The Gothic alphabet of Ulfilas is not less of Greek origin than the Cyrillian of the Slavs; nay, even the Runes are undoubtedly a form of development from the same source, having probably come at an early date to the Gauls by way of Massilia, and from them to the Teutons.[1] Professor Albrecht Weber has made a Semitic origin of the Indian Devanagari, too, appear very probable, whereby a great number of Asiatic systems of writing are referred to the same source, since not only the indigenous systems of Hindostan and Farther India, such as Bengali, Uriya, Telinga, Tamil, as well as the Burmese and Javanese systems, but also the Tibetan, are offsprings or sister-systems of the Devanagari. The writings of the Mongols, Tunguses, and Manchus, as Klaproth has already observed, are formed out of the Syrian by changing the horizontal into the upright position of the Chinese columns. If we add to these the still preserved characters of the fundamental Semitic alphabet itself in its Hebrew, Ethiopian, Samaritan, Zend or Middle Persian, Syrian, and Arabic branches, and if we further consider that the latter branch has been adopted by the Turks, Persians, Malays, and the Hindustani, we cannot but be astonished at the capability in such a discovery of being diffused from one point. Permit me only, for the sake of completeness, to mention the two youngest and

---

[1] Lauth, on the contrary, assumes the German Runes to have come from the Teutons to the Gauls, and at the same time gives a different and satisfactory explanation of the passage in Tacitus, which has been construed to imply the unacquaintance of the Germans with alphabetic writing, by referring it to a merely epistolary intercourse.

E

not least noteworthy scions of our alphabet, which are
not borrowed from it, but merely invented in imitation of
it from vague report, viz., the writing of the Cherokees,
invented by Sequoyah about 1823, and that of the
Negroes of the Vei country, dating ten years later, by
Doalu Bukere.   The two inventions present interesting
points of agreement.   Both the Indian and the African
inventor, by observing the epistolary intercourse of the
Europeans, were set to reflect on the possibility of
writing their mother tongue; both had an imperfect
knowledge of the English alphabet.   Neither of them set
up an alphabetic, but both a syllabic writing. Sequoyah,
indeed, had at first set up, as the Vei writing had, about
200 characters, but subsequently reduced them to 85.
Leaving these psychologically interesting phenomena
of the most recent times out of the question, of all
the modes of writing in use on the whole earth, only
the Chinese and the syllabic writing of the Japanese,
formed out of it, may be with certainty excluded from
the universal descent from the one Semitic alphabet.
But the ever-memorable discoveries of the present
century have made us acquainted, in the Egyptian
hieroglyphs, with a most remarkable antique parallel
to the Chinese; in various species of arrow-headed
writing with very complete alphabets; in the Assyrian
with an intermediate stage between word- and syllabic-
writing, promising the most important clues; and by
the side of these we have the hieroglyphs of the aborigines of America, being an as yet unsolved though not
insolvable problem.   Have we thus arrived at a last

and radical variety ?   Do the three systems of picture-writing of the Egyptians, Chinese, and Americans, the mixed system of the Assyrians, and, finally, the alphabetic writings of the Persians and Semites, offer us at least six independent solutions of the gigantic problem as to the exhibition of our ideas to the eye ?   Although the time for the final decision of this question has not yet arrived, I cannot forbear stating it as my conviction that such a sixfold origin of the most marvellous art which it was at all possible for man to create appears to me incredible.   Nay, from what has in other respects forced itself upon my mind as probable with regard to a primeval intercourse between the entire human race, the diffusion of that art from one common centre seems by no means impossible.   The original home of the alphabet destined to such wide dissemination was doubtless Babylon, which, since Professor Böckh, we have known to be the starting-point of the system of weights and measures universally adopted in antiquity, and come down thence to us, and the importance of which to astronomy and mathematics is perhaps not even yet sufficiently appreciated.   The names of the letters of the Hebrew alphabet are of Chaldean origin; at least the occurrence of the camel as the name of the third letter precludes our thinking of Palestine proper.   The Phœnicians may indeed have been the disseminators, but cannot have been the inventors, of the alphabet.   Although the connecting links are not yet discovered, according to all analogy hardly any one, considering the close vicinity, will be inclined to be-

lieve that the ancient Persian alphabetic writing should
have had a second independent origin. But I ask, did
this Persian mode of writing originate independently
of the varieties of the cuneiform writing connected with
it, especially independently of the Assyrian? Should
not Egypt have been able to influence Assyrian writing
in the earliest time, in the same way as at a later period
Assyrian influence on the hieroglyphs becomes percep-
tible? The similarity of the principle of Semitic writing
to that of the hieroglyphics, expressing as these do only
the initial consonant of the word represented in the
picture, was noticed already by Champollion at an early
date.[1]

On the other hand, the most ancient pictures, which,
according to Prof. Qppert, belong to a Scythian or Tura-
nian people, and from which the arrow-headed forms
are derived, have in them something that, as regards at
least their general impression, reminds one of the ancient Tchuen writing of the Chinese. Considered on the
whole, there is no reason why we should think a trans-
mission, at a very early period, of the rudiments of a
system of writing from one people and part of the earth
to another impossible. Nay, the traces discovered by

---

[1] Already, in his "Lettre à M. Dacier," Champollion expresses
himself clearly on this subject. He says, "J'oserai dire plus : il serait
possible de retrouver, dans cette ancienne écriture phonétique égyp-
tienne, quelque imparfaite qu'elle soit en elle-même, sinon l'origine,
du moins le modèle sur lequel peuvent avoir été calqués les alphabets
des peuples de l'Asie occidentale," &c. After dwelling upon the resemblance of the two systems, he arrives at the conclusion, and says :
"C'est dire enfin que l'Europe, qui reçut de la vieille Egypte les élé-
ments des sciences et des arts, lui devrait encore l'inappréciable bien-
fait de l'écriture alphabétique."

Alexander von Humboldt of an intercourse that once existed between Mexico and Eastern Asia do not even wholly exclude a migration of picture-writing as far as those parts. But as all this must still remain simply an hypothesis, we may meanwhile be quite satisfied with the inner unity which, so far as any mode of writing had a natural development, is everywhere conspicuous. It may perhaps be regarded as an acknowledged fact, which only does not always admit of proof owing to the lack of authorities to refer to, that every phonetic symbol springs from a pictorial representation. As every element of language, even derivative syllables at present all but meaningless, originally had its signification, so every letter was originally a picture. This statement, however, must not be understood to imply that writing once originated in a species of painting, or that the first representation of man's ideas were paintings. Even if we leave all secondary employments of Chinese and Egyptian hieroglyphics out of consideration, and assume a period when writing consisted only of the sensuous copies of things, such as a man, the sun, a bird, it does not on that account become—what misconception has to this day made of the Mexican—the total representation of an event intended for the eye instead of for the mind. That writing is a symbol for language, has been already said by Aristotle, and the definition is verified by the hieroglyphics up to their very first origin. Even where the word and the thing coincide, the picture is only the symbol of the word: it is intended

to awaken language, to remind us of a sound, not of a
thing; to speak through the eye to the ear, not immediately to reason.   Writing, in fact, is not an object for
mute contemplation; it wants reading—loud reading.
Not like figures in a painting, but as words are co-
ordinated to sentences, so must these pictures be combined to the totality of an action.   They also represent
the symbolised word to the whole extent of its idea,
and not only from its symbolised side.   Or can it be
supposed that the Chinese picture for the sun ever
signified the word *shi* only in the sense of sun and
not likewise in that of day?   That is quite impossible.
Precisely in the earliest time man with his whole
reason was so completely under the dominion of the
word, that necessarily a picture would signify what
its name was, and be understood as it sounded when
read.

It is well known in what way the hieroglyphics
could dwindle down to phonetic symbols, aye, even
to mere letters.   But in their earliest form they invariably denoted words, never anything more.   The
fundamental law of the development of writing is the
gradually growing independence of the sound, while
at first sound and conception are represented as not
divorced from each other.   Of course not every word
comes at once to be represented; those have prece-
dence the conception of which, from its corresponding
to something shaped, invites representation.   Already
at an early period the word-pictures contained more
than could be conveyed in a drawing which had to

start from a far more limited object than the conception of the word in all its bearings. The process of painting in words conquers a wider territory for the meanings of a sign: it gives the same sound a wider scope, seeking for conceptions which seem to coincide with what it originally denotes.

The first mode, however, of *multiplying* signs by the representation of such words as, after the invention of word-pictures—which are to writing what roots are to language—had been brought to an end, had not fitted in with any of those extant, was that of forming collective pictures by juxtaposition. The Chinese simple pictures 日 *shi*, "sun," and 月 *yue*, "moon," signify when placed together, the word *ming*, "lustre" (日月). It can hardly be supposed that we have here the abstract idea of lustre as a quality of both heavenly bodies presented to us; but the first meaning represented was undoubtedly morning, being the time when the sun is seen in the heavens simultaneously with the moon,— the meeting of day and night. Thus the morning-star is called *'ki-ming* (日月 尾火 Shi-King, ii. 5, 9), properly speaking, "opening the morning," *ming-shi*, "to-morrow;" and the employment of the word for the future likewise proceeds from this meaning. Another representation of the idea of morning is the picture of the word *tán*, "morning, day," 旦 , representing the sun above the horizon. If below this sign that of the moon too is placed, so that the latter is represented as below, the sun as above, the horizon, there arises 朝 the

picture of the word *yāng*, "sunrise, bright sky, brightness." But the sun above the moon, 昴, signifies the
word *ĭ*, "change," which *e.g.*, is met with in the name
of the book I-King. The sign evidently represents the
moon as alternating with the sun, that is to say, the
alternation of day and night. The first phonetic signs
seem to have proceeded from an enlarged use of the
pictures for homonymous words, similar in idea but
yet distinguishable.[1] The sign 青 for *tsing*, signifying
the blue and green colours, combined with the sign 艹
for *thsao*, "plant," form the nearly homonymous word
tsîng, "flourishing, luxuriant" (Shi, ii. 3, 2), and with the
米 for *mĭ*, "rice, food," the 米 青 for *'tsîng*, "ripe, full
grown, finished, able." The pictures for "growth" or for
"rice" certainly never denoted the words *tsîng*, *'tsîng ;*
but it is probable that the sign representing colour was
also once used for them, and only subsequently received
the explanatory supplement defining the idea. The
same holds good of 氵青 *'tsîng*, "pure," of fluids (Shi, ii.
5, 10, 6, 6; iii. 1, 5; iv. 3, 2), which is combined with
the notional sign 氵 for water. We must not imagine
that a character ever proceeded from an idea without

---

[1] Professor Steinthal, too ("The Development of Writing," p. 94),
finds the bridge between notional and phonetic writing "where the
identity of the sound of two words coincides with a cognate signification." The description of the phonetic element of Egyptian and
Chinese writing and its development is perhaps the most beautiful,
and, according to my conviction, most successful, portion of that brilliant treatise.

regard to the sound, since the remoter the period, the more the former was extant in the latter only for the conception, and the mind was chained to the word. Not the designation of the sound, but its independent designation, detached from the idea, forms the essential feature of the higher stage of writing. All that we know of the nature of Mexican writing shows us that it is subject to the same laws. The same difference that we observe between the Egyptian pictures and the hieroglyphics accompanying them is equally to be remarked among the Mexican. Even as regards the Chinese characters, it took a long time before Europe came to know to what extent they are phonetic writing. The French missionaries, who read these characters with ease, who understood the language in which they are written, who lived in the country where they were constantly employed and where the principle of their composition was perfectly understood, entertained, nevertheless, the most erroneous ideas of their figurative signification. It was reserved for M. Abel Rémusat to disseminate more correct notions on this subject. What trouble it cost to gain the conviction that the Egyptian hieroglyphics have a phonetic value, how isolated and obscure are the utterances on this matter of the elder writers down to Champollion, who, in his turn, was aided by the light thrown on Chinese writing and justly often refers to it, is notorious. We need certainly, therefore, not wonder at Spanish writers who represent Mexican picture-writing as consisting of actual paintings. But it is with this exactly as with the two other modes of writing similar to it. On a closer inspection we find in all of them the contrast to ours indeed great enough, but not so absolute as at first sight it appeared. We find the true and irreconcilable contrast between writing and painting by no means annulled in them; the picture represents the thing while writing represents the word, and in this sense the hieroglyphics of the Mexicans, as well as those of the Egyptians and Chinese, are, no doubt, writing and not pictures. What, therefore, we may designate as the real invention of writing would have been the collection of a limited cycle of pictures of visible objects, each of which reminds us equally of the word, *i.e.*, the name of the object. Here writing certainly coincides with drawing, but not in such a way as to necessitate our believing there had previously existed an independent, non-symbolical employment of painting. Language points to a reversed way : the German *malen*, as derived from Gothic *meljan*, primarily signifies "to write;" of γράφω the same holds good. The Slavonic *pisatj*, to whose affinity with the *nipistam* of the Persian inscriptions Professor Spiegel has drawn attention, signified already among the two Indo-European peoples "to write," while the Greek ποικίλος, and the well-known corresponding Sanskrit words refer to colour. But, I would ask, what was the object of these ancient drawings, and what gave rise to them? It is plain that this question is inseparable from that as to the earliest employment of writing, its subject-matter, and even the material

on which people wrote. And here, again, language
affords us a momentous hint. It is well known that
a great number of the words signifying "to write" can
be proved to be derived from the signification "to
scratch." Γράφω and *scribo*, the English *to write*, the
Northern *rista runir*, to scratch Runes, our *reissen*,
Riss, are obvious examples. The same may be said
of the Sanskrit root *likh*. The earliest writing was
scratched. But on what? We see it in the remotest
antiquity engraved on rocks and applied to sacred monu-
mental purposes. But there are also numerous testimonies to the process of scratching in wood, and this
seems the more likely as regards the primitive time at
which the very first beginnings of writing took their
origin. I would remind you of the Chinese wood-tablets
which are mentioned in the Shi-King (ii. 8), where a
warrior laments, saying, " Why should I not think of my
return home ? But I fear the writing on this tablet,"
i.e., the command written on a wooden tablet. Still
simpler and as numerously testified is the process of
writing on the bark of trees, especially on that of the
birch. Pliny (xvi. 13) gives an account of the proceed-
ings of spies who carve letters, which are at first invisible, in the fresh bark of trees. In our German *Lache*
we have a special word for a sign carved in a tree ;
it is probably related to the Sanskrit root *likh*. In
"Vikramorvasi" we meet with a passage spoken of in
Professor Max Müller's "History of Ancient Sanskrit
Literature," where Urvasi writes a love-letter on a

birch leaf, *i.e.*, a leaf of birch bark. Even in "Simpli-
cissimus" we still read of a book written on birch
bark. But if we inquire more searchingly into the
motives that may have determined the people in
primitive times to supersede with such consistency
as, at least, etymology renders it probable, so simple
a process as the spreading of colour by carving, and
altogether if we seriously ask ourselves what might
have been their immediate motive for writing or
drawing, we shall perhaps be induced to go a step
farther guided by language. A closer observation of
nearly all the words used for the idea of writing
seems to go a considerable way towards proving
that the writing material which floated, as it were,
before language in bestowing these appellations was
no other than the human body; in other words, that
writing has developed from tattooing. The special
direction which the development of the meaning has
in each case taken is a subject never to be neglected
in tracing the historical root of a word-notion. Thus,
e.g., it would be insufficient to have set up in γράφω,
"to write," a general primary meaning of "to grave,"
and we should be even absolutely wrong if we
attempted to find the connecting link between the
two ideas in stone or wood writing. For the Greek
word has its definite history; before it acquired its
special meaning to write, it already had a special
signification, which was not that of chiselling and
hewing of stone and wood, but quite distinctly the

scratching into the skin. Its idea is in the first instance connected, not indeed with *sculpo*, γλύφω, but with *scalpo* and γλάφω. Homer seven times uses the word with its derivations of slight wounds caused by missiles, of hurts in the skin, grazing or flaying, also of scratching with thorns; once, too, ἐπιγράφω occurs in the "Iliad" of the sign which is scratched on the lot; once γράφω in the much-discussed passage (vi. 167 *sq.*) where Proitos "dreads indeed to kill Bellerophon, but sends him to Lycia, giving him sad signs, after having scratched many fatal ones on a folded tablet, which he commands him to show his father-in-law, so that he may perish." The reference to the skin, moreover, is still extant in the later word γράπτης, "wrinkled." To the word γριφᾶσθαι, which Professor Benfey very correctly places by the side of *scribo*, "to write," Hesychius ascribes the additional meanings in the Laconic dialect of "to scrape" and "pluck" (ξύειν, σκύλλειν). The Hebrew *sefer*, "writing," may in the same way be explained by the Chaldean *sappar*, "to shear," *mispera*, "shears," for which, according to all analogy, we may assume the scraping of the skin to have been the fundamental idea. The word *katab*, common to the Semitic family, occurs at such an early date as Semitic writing is mentioned at all (Lev. xix. 28), in the prohibition "not to print any marks upon" the skin, and the *ketobet* there used seems to be a derivative expressly intended to convey the sense of tattooing, which is thereby at the same time indicated as, according to all appearance, a religious practice among the Semitic peoples.[1]

The word "tattoo" is borrowed from the Marquesas dialect of the Oceanic family of languages, its form there being *tatu.* In the language of the Sandwich

---

[1] In connection with the above lecture, Professor Fleischer has added from the *Arabic* a considerable number of examples of the transition of the idea from scratching to writing, but expressed his dissent with regard to the derivation of *kataba* from the same fundamental idea, and, comparing it with *katĭbatun,* "army," *kattaba,* "collecting such a one, levying"—though it is to be presumed without associating with it the idea of conscription—assumed for it the signification of *joining, stringing together.* I will not attempt to oppose such a meaning of the root in question, and am ready to acknowledge that the parallel quoted by Professor Fleischer is well worthy of attention. Yet, apart from the consideration that the words quoted might be kept wholly distinct from the root signifying "to write," a root having two quite different significations being notoriously nothing uncommon in Semitic languages, two further explanations appear to me admissible. First, the meaning "host" might equally with the German word *Schar* be derived from "separating" as well as from "joining," and go back to the primary sense of "scratching" assumed for *kataba,* which would be connected with *qaṣab,* "to split, to shear," *chaṣab,* "to carve," *e.g.,* writing on rocks, and the like. But, secondly, there are some positive instances in which the idea of *counting* proceeds from that of *writing, i.e.,* in the sense of "making strokes." Thus the Kafir word *bala* signifies to "write," "count," and "reckon," and finally, too, to "relate;" and yet the words here formed of the root with the meanings of "sign," "stain," "colour," show writing to be the fundamental idea. Döhne in his Zulu Kafir Dictionary (Cape Town, 1857) expresses himself on this subject on the whole very correctly thus: "The original idea of writing and numbering with the Kafir was that of representing things by a simple figure, and coincides with those of other nations. If a description of a thing was to be given, a certain shape, form, stroke, or line was made in the sand, or in the ground. These were the signs for both writing and numbering, every new number being represented by another stroke or mark. Or, if this practice was not convenient for counting, one finger of the hand was raised instead of a stroke in the ground. The sense of writing is, therefore, primary, and that of counting secondary." Compare with this, too, the above-mentioned

Islands *k* is substituted for the missing *t;* the word *kakau,* "to write," belonging to it, does not therefore materially differ from *tatu.* In the language of the Marquesas itself, too, *tatau* means "to read, cipher, draw." Another word, common to both dialects, with

significations "to reckon," "to draw," in the word *tatau* of the Marquesas Islands. The *analogy of ideas* here quoted from quite distant spheres of language, on the nature of which in general I beg to refer the reader to the first volume of my work, "Ursprung und Entwickelung der menschlichen Sprache und Vernunft" ("On the Origin and Evolution of Human Speech and Reason," Stuttgart, J. G. Cotta, 1868)—the above lecture is only an abridged extract from a chapter of the as yet unpublished second volume—seems to me important, too, for the history of the Hebrew root *safar,* of which Fürst justly lays down *three* principal meanings in the following order :—1. To incise, write ; 2. to count, appropriately to make incisions, marks ; and 3. to relate. While, namely, *safar* means only "to count," and *sipper* (in the Piel), "to count" and "relate" (subsequently also "to speak," *e.g.,* "Adam spoke Aramean," Synh. 38b.), and the substantive derivation *mispar* and some others less in use convey the same meaning, *sefer* mostly signifies "book," often, too, "document, letter,"in some passages the material on which was written, besides absolutely "writing," τὰ γράμματα, *e.g.,* "to teach the writing and language of the Chaldeans" (Dan. i. 4) ; the prophet Isaiah expresses "to know to read" (xxix. 11, 12) by *yadá sefer.* The sense of "register," which the word, Gen. v. 1, may be taken to bear, is intermediate between to count and write ; and the same applies to the remarkable word *sofer.* This word evidently denoted the dignitary whom we find represented on Egyptian and Assyrian monuments with the writing tablet or scroll in the act of recording, and might therefore be translated by "writer" as well as by "teller, recorder." In the post-biblical language the word appears in quite a different meaning, viz., as *scholar.* Only with reference to Ezra we meet with this signification also in several biblical passages. Should it here be only a change made in the spirit of the time in the case of Ezra's title, which perhaps he had brought with him from Babylon in quite a different sense ? For the rest, the honourable title in the passages in question seems only intended to express that Ezra was able to read well (see especially Neh. viii. and Ezra vii. 6) ; at most perhaps that he was well read (*litteratus*), *i.e.,* in the law ; and I would here render it rather by "reader" than "scribe" (*i.e.,* writer).

a slight variation, is *tiki*—in the Sandwich Islands, *kiki*—"to tattoo, paint, write." It also means "carved image," in which sense it springs from "token" (sign), like *signum*. A New Zealand tomb, too, an illustration of which is given in Hochstetter's "Neuseeland"

The meaning "scholar," doubtless proceeds from *sefer* in the sense of writing, art of reading ; a "scholar" was originally he that could read and write, for this earliest import of grammar and the grammarian (γραμματική, γραμματικός) was for some time the sum total of all erudition. When matters changed, *sofer* not only received the idea of learned man (scribe, γραμματεύς), but even that of elementary teacher, as conveyed by the Greek word γραμματιστής ; nay, as the once rare learning had passed on to the children, we meet even with a Talmudic passage (of the third century) where the Abecedarians are called *Soferim* (Kidd. iv. 13). Another Talmudical passage (Kidd. 30) derives this (at that time obsolete) appellation of the "former" scholars from the signification "to count," *i.e.*, as of those who had counted the letters of the law. In the latest Hebrew, *sofer* means scribe (*scriba, notarius*), copyist (of the law, religious documents, &c.). Now, as regards *katab*, this root does not occur in Genesis, as, indeed, it is significant that before the exodus from Egypt writing is not spoken of in the Bible, and even *sefer* only in the passage quoted above (Gen. v. 1), in the sense of register. Subsequently *katab*, as is well known, is the ordinary verbal root for to write, with which the substantive *sefer* is very frequently connected. But there are also some few passages in which the verb signifies nothing but to *count*, especially Isa. x. 19, "And the rest of the trees of his forest shall be few, that a child may count (write) them," where *mispar* too, in the first half of the verse, properly speaking, means as much as "what can be counted." Again, "The Lord shall count (*yispor*), when he writeth up the people, that this man was born there" (Ps. lxxxvii. 6). Such a use of *katab* no doubt proceeds from counting by strokes, not from a more complicated notation. If in the first quoted passage the writing of the number in Hebrew letters was perhaps to be conveyed, we have to consider that in them 400 is easier to write than 11, and not much more difficult than 1. Accordingly the Arabic *katibatun* too might go back to such a primitive counting in writing and simply mean "number," the rather as the *sofer* of the ancient Hebrew writings, too, had principally to note down the army (see particularly Isa. lii. 25, 2 Kings xxv. 19, 2 Chron. xxvi. 11). Indeed counting by strokes is to be traced back to as early a date as writing in general, and even the employment of the letters of the alphabet as figures was introduced along with it in Europe.

(p. 201), was pointed out to him by the natives by the designation of *tiki*. As regards the original significa-tion of *tiki*, we gather it from *tikao*, " to sting, irritate," *tikaue*, " gnat," *tikao* and *tiko-tiko*, " sensual pleasure." According to Wilhelm von Humboldt's statement in " Ueber die Verschiedenheit des menschlichen Sprach-baus " (On the Variety of Structures of Human Languages," p. 406), Jacquet observes " that among those tribes the ideas of writing and tattooing are closely connected."

In Zimmermann's " Dictionary of the Gang Language," which is spoken by a tribe on the Gold Coast of West Africa, the root *nma* is explained by *.*"to scratch "— *e.g.*, the face—" to make strokes or signs, to write." In the Burmese language *koh* (according to Schleier-macher) means "to scratch," as children do, and "to write." The same transition is found in the Kafir word *loba*.

In order to find a similar connection of the two ideas among the ancient civilised nations probable, we should remember the testimony we have to the early and widely diffused practice of marking the body with signs scratched in. Tattooing itself occurs among the savage tribes in Europe and Asia, as well as in the more recently discovered parts of the earth. Of the Kabyls it is reported that, by way of dis-tinguishing their tribes, they wear pictures of animals on the forehead, nose, temples, or on one of the cheeks ; such tattooing is done by puncturing the skin with fine needles dipped in a caustic fluid. A similar process is

F

met with everywhere in Central Africa, as well as in the Caroline Archipelago. "Tattooing," says Herodotus (v. 6), speaking of the Thracians, "is considered aristocratic; non-tattooed people are looked down upon as ignoble." Xenophon gives a somewhat more minute description of the same practice among the Mosynoekoi (An. v. 4, 32). He says, "They showed us pampered children of aristocratic parents, who had been fed with boiled chestnuts; they were very delicate and white, and nearly as stout as they were tall; their backs and fronts were tattooed, the former in gaudy colours, the latter all over with marks." Also on the Egyptian monuments of Biban-el-Moluk tattooed men are found depicted. Among the Greeks and Romans, as we learn from Petronius (Sat. c. 103 *sqq.*), it was a common practice to brand criminals and slaves, for which latter it seems to have been originally introduced; and equally so among the Persians, of whom Herodotus (vii. 233) reports they had, at Xerxes' orders, branded with the royal mark the Theban deserters at Thermopylæ. This practice, which had no other intention but that of distinguishing by some mark, proceeded from tattooing. At all events, we are wrong in giving the Greek word a different sense, especially that of an actual burning in of the mark. It is, in fact, the στίζω used for tattooing in the passages quoted. The corresponding punishment of the Chinese has adhered to this original form. It consists in pricking with a needle marks in the flesh of the culprit and then making them durable by a black dye. This process, which

closely resembles tattooing, is called *thsi*, 刺, and
khing, 京刂, 劓, 黥. The Manchu word
for it is *sabsimbi* (according to von der Gabelentz),
"to brand, to tattoo, and a work with the needle."
Perhaps the idea of acupuncture, which in times im-
memorial the Chinese employed as a remedy, is likewise to be traced to the tattooing process, so far as
it might be regarded as holy and salutary. Horses
were notoriously provided among the Greeks with
marks branded in their haunches for the purpose of
distinguishing their breed. For this object characters
were employed, and their being thus employed was
probably as old a practice among the Greeks as alphabetic writing itself; at least the letter *koppa*, that
so early ceased to be used in writing, was among
those characters. The Caucasians have to this day
a complete and abundant alphabet of signs which
likewise serve no other purpose but that of distinguishing their horses.

The Biblical expression, "I will not forget thee
(Zion); I have graven thee upon the palms of my
hands; thy walls are continually before me" (Isa. xlix.
15, 16), may, perhaps, remind us of the practice of
tattooing. Equally so the well - known incident
reported by Herodotus (v. 35), that Histiæus, with
a view by stealth to summon Aristagoras to revolt,
shaved a slave, wrote the missive on his head, and,
his hair having grown again, despatched him on his
errand, points to a sphere of ideas which is not un-

accustomed to regard the human body as writing material. It only remains to be mentioned as noteworthy that Herodotus in the passage cited uses the word ἔστιξε, which proceeds from the idea of tattooing or puncturing. With respect to form, writing presents no contrast to tattooing. Some tribes mark their skin with figures of animals of the most various kinds. Such marks are in form regular pictures like the earliest writing. Mostly, however, the marks scratched in the flesh are linear. Hochstetter says of the sepulchral monuments of the Maoris, the aborigines of New Zealand (" Neuseeland," p. 299), " They are figures four feet high, carved out of wood, round which are hung garments or cloths, and on which the faithful imitation of the tattooed lines on the face of the deceased is the most remarkable feature. By them the Maori knows to whom the monument is erected. Certain lines denote the name, others the family to which the deceased belonged, and others again the person himself. Close imitation of tattooing in the face, therefore, is to the Maori tantamount to the likeness of a portrait, and he requires no further inscription to know what chief lies buried underneath." The style of drawing here is linear, and it is noteworthy that the words used for " writing " likewise generally have the primary sense of *making strokes.* From the Greek γράφω, *e.g.,* the idea of " line," " stroke," γράμμη, is developed in as direct a manner as " writing " and " picture."

A curious relic of genuine tattooing has been preserved amidst our very civilisation. Among Euro-

pean sailors, and partly, too, among soldiers, regular
gaudy tattooing is still practised. The operation
is performed by experts with an instrument quite
similar to that described by Cook, viz., composed of
stuck-up needles. In this way sailors or soldiers have
their arms and chests marked with symbols of their
profession; sometimes, too, regular writing is used.
This is doubtless an imitation of savage tribes.

In some words used to convey the idea of writing,
there is a certain vacillation between the primary sense
of scratching in and dyeing. This may, perhaps, be
accounted for by the fact that tattooing implied both
together, and, by aid of the blood flowing from the
wound, did so from the very first. From man's own
body the characters were probably next transferred to
objects to which they were applied as marks. It is even
reported that some Indian tribes, for the purpose of
preserving their pedigrees, carved, in the order of their
succession, the so-called *totem*, *i.e.*, symbolic pictures
of their tribes, for which they employed figures of
animals, such as the bear, buffalo, and the like, in
trees, oars, canoes, and weapons. This is already a
kind of writing for the mere purpose of recording, without reference to the material on which the writing
is carried on. The walls of Egyptian temples and
palaces, owing to the mass of characters with which
they were covered, have been likened to books; the
inscriptions on the mighty rocks at Persepolis and
Bisitun contain entire histories; why should not, in a
ruder stage, a like use be made of trees and animals?

The loosening of the bark, with writing upon it, from a tree, the stripping of the skin, furnished with marks, from an animal, would be, at the same time, the first step towards rendering the writing independent, —the production of the first book, as it were. Among the New Zealanders, who have adopted an alphabet of fourteen letters from the English, the custom at present prevails of writing their names or greetings to their friends with shells on the leaves of flax bushes. "The Dinka negroes," as Mitterrutzner reports, "often scratch or carve with a thorn or pointed iron on soft pumpkin shells the rough outlines of human beings, crocodiles, tortoises, and other animals. This mode of graving they call *gor*. When they happened to see a missionary write, they would say *jen a gor*, he engraves, scratches in, draws." The most ancient relics of Chinese writing that are still preserved are inscriptions on consecrated vessels, and in so far as the inscription was presumably intended as a mark of the utmost durability, a satisfactory explanation is afforded why at first it was not written on, but graven in, the vessels. An analogous conception seems to have been at all times associated with the idea of " sign : " *signum*, *e.g.*, as Professor George Curtius has justly inferred from *sigillum*, was primarily an engraved sign. Ebel has explained it from *stignum*, and has unnecessarily, I think, subsequently withdrawn this ingenious explanation; for *signum* would in that case be related not only to the Gothic *taikns*, the English *token*, our *Zeichen*, but also to *stechen* (to sting) and στίζω, the genuine Greek designation for tattooing, mentioned above. That *zeich-nen* (to design) was derived from *Zeichen* (sign), and *dessiner* from *signum*, shows us anew the symbolic purpose at first associated with designing. An object, an animal, a man was *designed*, that is, provided with a sign which made it recognisable, marked it as a possession or consecrated it. There is a consecration by the impression of a sign still more primitive than that just described, and the purpose of which is at the same time transparent enough: I mean the so-called *red hand* of the Indians. Schoolcraft has found it depicted as a holy emblem on bark, on hides of animals, on wooden tablets, but also on the bodies of dancers. In the latter case the picture was produced by the print of a hand smeared with clay on the chest, the shoulder, and other parts of the body. What this hand, so universal among the Indian tribes, may mean, will scarcely remain doubtful to any one who has seen the radiant hands of the sun-god on Egyptian representations, or read in the Veda hymns of the golden-handed Savitri. The red, or sometimes white, hand, with which an object, and even the body of a man, is painted and consecrated in the most simple manner, is hardly aught else but the sun.

Long as the way may seem from such a sign, impressed almost like an incidental animal trace, up to our alphabet of twenty-four letters, in which the faint remnant of a hand denotes simply the sound *i* or *j*, yet I believe the origin of writing may be explained in this manner without leaving too wide gaps. To scratch in signs with a view to making them permanent, to multiply them, to employ them more especially on monuments, to make use of them as phonetic signs, to arrange them into a kind of system, as was done by one or several gifted tribes, these are steps which betoken indeed an admirable but no longer an absolutely marvellous progress. Equally the transition from an Egyptian system of hieroglyphics to real alphabetic writing is certainly by no means inconceivable. The latest form of Egyptian writing, the so-called Demotic, though only its last abbreviation in current hand, produces outwardly the impression of an alphabetic writing, and was considered as such before people ventured to seek for a phonetic principle in the hieroglyphics. It is to that impression, and to the decipherment under its dominion by De Sacy and Akerblad in the first instance, that we owe that of the hieroglyphics too, and the resuscitation of the language and primeval history of Egypt in general. As to the nature and the application of the hieroglyphic symbols, we must consider that the employment of the hieroglyphs which comes nearest that of alphabetic writing, viz., that where the initial sound has a value, happens to be indisputably the practice in foreign names, and that the Egyptians, if they had wished to make use of their writing for a Semitic language, would certainly have done so according to that principle. The great step to a real alphabetic writing consists in the latter having only one sign for a sound, whereas hieroglyphic writing, even when it proceeds strictly on the alphabetic principle, has always the option left between various pictures. Without the reduction of phonetic hieroglyphics to the smallest number possible, the alphabet would have had many hundreds of letters instead of twenty-two, and this reduction would therefore be what we may allow to pass for the invention of alphabetic writing. Those acquainted with Egyptian writing are aware that supports for such a simplification exist in hieroglyphic orthography itself, which, by the way, far from having been a conscious choice, may perhaps have been the outcome of a development extending over many centuries.

If, instead of starting from an entirely instinctive origin of writing, wholly unconscious of its final purposes, we were to set human ingenuity the task of creating this wonderful art, we should encounter the same impossibility as when we would make language originate in human reason and reflection. If language were an invention, the wisdom of man previous to such invention would have been infinitely superior to what it is at present. As in language, so in writing too, with all the intellect displayed in it, though it was developed in what was already nearly the historical period, we cannot recognise a production of the intellect itself, but only one of those instinctive creations of the human mind which, though results of an irrational evolution, conceal within them the highest and most admirable symptoms of reason, exactly as do the marvels of nature that surround us.

V.

The Discovery of Fire.

[A Lecture delivered at the Museum Club at Frankfort-on-the-Maine, March 25, 1870.]

AMONG the blessings which man from the earliest times called his own, some are so indispensable to him, aye, so inseparable from his nature, that it is easier for him to believe he has possessed them from all time than to form any conception of how he may have acquired them. The most universal of these purely human blessings, language, still lies within the sphere of the forces of nature. If its possession by man ever had a beginning, it could only have come to him by nature, but could not have been discovered or invented by him. But it is different with those blessings that he owes to culture. Impossible as, for instance, it is to ascribe alphabetic writing to a conscious invention, seeing that such an invention would presuppose a superhuman wisdom by which the inventor perceived that all our speech is only a thousand-fold combination of twenty-four sounds; yet writing cannot have developed without the aid of reflection. Man is perhaps by nature a speaking being, certainly not a writing one. In a still higher degree this holds

good of material productions, of implements and tools
with which the human race has supplied and improved
its existence. ⌈ Each of these implements must, in however rude a condition, have once become serviceable to
man for the first time ; the idea of its utility must once
have dawned upon some generation or another ; and
however great the difference may be between a steam-
engine of our day and the earliest stone hammer, the
being who for the first time armed his hand with such
a tool, and in this way for the first time perhaps beat
the kernel of a fruit out of its hard shell, must, it would
appear, have felt within him a breath of that inspiration which a discoverer in our own time feels when a
new idea flashes upon him. And in this sense, I suppose, we may venture to call the preparation of artificial fire an invention, a discovery, though the same
rule applies to fire as to all the characteristically distinctive acquisitions of man as compared to the brute, viz.,
their being in fact too great, of too momentous consequences to the fortunes of the race, not to make it
appear doubtful whether we may trace them back to a
human origin, to a discovery of the human mind.

Fire belongs to those distinctive possessions of man,
such as tools and implements, language and religion,
without which we cannot conceive of humanity.
All the reports about tribes who were said not to
have any knowledge of it have proved fables, nay,
inconceivable. But surely it is no less inconceivable
for an animal to make fire itself, or even to avail itself
of it. Its effect on the higher brute creation is terror

the wolf, the lion, the elephant, are kept aloof from the encampments of man by fire. And if we admire in genius not only a superior intellectual endowment but the boldness of attempting to think of what has never been thought of by any one before, and to undertake what has never been done before, it was surely an act of genius when man approached the dreaded glow, when he bore the flame before him over the earth on the top of the ignited log of wood—an act of daring without a prototype in the animal world, and in its consequences for the development of human culture truly immeasurable. If antiquity beheld in that hero of the well-known legend, in Prometheus, who brought down fire from heaven, the author of all culture, we who live in the age of industry, we to whom fire is the substitute for millions of hands and horse power, will probably be inclined to rate such a boon still more highly. But in the domain of material progress we are too much accustomed to that great feat of man to think we need for the beginnings of the history of our civilisation the aid of gods or demigods; we rather seek for a motive which might in some measure resemble the powerful and intelligent industry of our times, and (singularly enough in the case of a thing having such an infinite variety of uses as fire) we shall be forced to acknowledge that such a motive, a practical reason for meditating the invention, or even for endeavouring to get possession of fire for practical application, can scarcely have existed in primeval times.

It is easy to think of an accidental impulse, perhaps

of an object set fire to by a flash of lightning or a
forest-fire, which may for the first time have thrown
the flame of itself, as it were, into the hands of man,
who would then soon have learned to avail himself of it. But though little weight may be attached
to the observation, it is notwithstanding to be taken
into consideration that such accidents are least likely
to have happened in those very places where there was
most occasion for really making use of the fire thus
presented to man. For it is precisely a warm climate
or a hot temperature which particularly favours such
accidents, and it hardly admits of doubt that the original home of the human race is to be looked for in hot
regions, if not even in the torrid zone itself, in the
vicinity of the equator. But what did he care there
for the flame generated by lightning? No necessity
rendered it worth his while to preserve it. It could
not be the preparation of his food which made fire a
desirable object to him; he must have for a long time
subsisted without such preparation, and without the
experience or any suspicion that fire might aid him
in it. Naturalists are not agreed as to whether the
earliest food of man was animal or merely vegetable.
Historically and linguistically considered, I, for my
own part, certainly deem it indubitable that, since man
has been man, he has been carnivorous. It is perhaps
not nature to which we may appeal when we kill
animals for the purpose of our own preservation; it
is perhaps only habit which makes this food appear
indispensable to us at present. In ancient times, and

still more in India, serious objections were notoriously raised to it; and even among us, the more sympathisingly we try to understand the animal soul, the more regretfully we feel this habit to be repugnant to our more tender volition; but we cannot deny that it is at any rate a very old habit, as is evident from the circumstance that notions such as *flesh, body*, and perhaps *animal* too, almost everywhere proceed from that of food; that language, therefore, decidedly presupposes animal food, and that since any such words have existed at all such food must have been common.

Not only are our own word *Fleisch* and the English *meat* derived from roots signifying "to eat," but also the French word *chair* is so derived, though according to the present usage of the language it happens not to imply meat as food. The noble Greek word *sarx*, which forms the first component in " sarcophagus," originally meant nothing but a morsel picked off. When we speak of a sarcastic smile, we have no idea how this epithet can be connected with the *sarx* just mentioned, nor could the Greeks themselves tell. Sarcasm, properly speaking, is not the subtle irony which we designate by it; it is a grin, a distortion of the mouth, or a showing one's teeth, and this forms the transition to the idea of pulling at a piece of meat with the teeth, whence that designation meat, which has become quite honourable in Greek by usage, has developed. At Logon in Central Africa, *thā* means "food," *thu* "meat," and *thă* "ox." Among other African tribes there exists only one word for meat and animal, and fish is called " water-flesh."

And what words allow us to guess agrees with all
that we know of the mode of life of savage tribes in
times past and present. Man in the most barbarous
state subsists everywhere by hunting, and only occasionally by catching fish; from the chase only he
passes on to a nomadic life and the breeding of cattle.
But it would be premature, from the indisputable pre-
ponderance of meat as food in prehistoric times, to
infer a preparation by fire. To this day some Indian
tribes—*e.g.*, in Florida—consume the booty they bring
home from the chase raw, and of the Huns it is notoriously reported that they knew how to soften their
meat without fire. There is no trace to be found in
language of such a preparation having preceded the
enjoyment of meat as food. What in this respect can
be more deceptive than our word *Braten* (roast)? Who
should doubt that it really implied something roasted?
And yet it does not. We have here one of those
curious, puzzling words before us which convey to
us quite a different sense from what they did to
their first inventors. *Braten* in the older language
signified nothing but "meat" and "flesh." It is not
derived from the verb *braten* (to roast) as now in
use, but from a homonymous root signifying "to eat,"
and which is also found in *Wildpret* (game). *Brot*
(bread) is derived from the same root, and observation
will show that appellations of bread often consist in
such words as in earlier times signified meat. If
we cast a glance at the various employments of fire
in the preparation of food in their historical succes-

sion, we shall find boiling to be the latest mode. In
the South Sea islands a preliminary step towards
it has been met with in the stewing of viands in
pits heated by red-hot stones. The earliest and most
direct preparation was the process of roasting, and
even Homer knew as yet of no other for the repasts
of his heroes. Nor was grain-fruit by any means
always baked, but for a long time consumed only in
roasted grains, as, *e.g.*, they have been found in pile-
dwellings. Language leads one step farther. The
root from which our word *kochen* (to boil) is derived
shows in cognate languages not only the idea of roasting but that of sun-burning, as well as that of the
ripening and mellowing of fruits and their becoming
eatable ; and equally so the Mexican *icuxitia*, "to boil,"
is derived from *icuci*, "to ripen." Such traces indicate
a time lying still within the development of language
when fire was not yet used as a medium between the
productions of the forest and the field and man's necessity for food.

What event may first have opened man's eyes and
pointed out to him a means by which he learned in so
many respects to render himself independent of the un-
friendliness of surrounding Nature ? It is certain that
not only the frost, but even more, perhaps, want of food,
would have prevented him from populating the earth
beyond his original home if he had not understood
how to recognise in the most formidable of elements
a beneficent power, and to make it do, in an enlarged
sphere, the work of the sun, which had till then warmed

and partly, too, nourished him. Though history seems to leave us in the dark on the cause of so momentous a change in man's mode of life, yet we have at our command very extensive and significant observations on the way in which artificial fire was produced, and there is every reason to suppose that we still have even the original, the really earliest, mode of making fire before us in the process adopted by many rude tribes. Among the Botocudos in Brazil as among some North American tribes, among the Greenlanders and in New Zealand, in Kamtshatka as among the Hottentots, the practice of producing fire by twirling or drilling two pieces of wood has been uniformly met with. The simplest, but also the most troublesome and time-wasting, process is that of placing a stick of wood perpendicularly on another lying horizontally, and rapidly turning it like a twirling-rod between the palms of the hands until the loosened shavings catch fire and ignite slips of bast kept in readiness.

If the employment of this apparatus for fire-making in parts so distant from each other is already calculated to excite some surprise, what shall we say when we find it used in earlier times, even in Arabia, China, India, Greece, Italy, nay, even in Germany? It is a merit due to comparative mythology to have proved the existence of the friction apparatus for producing fire in the Indo-European primeval times, *i.e.*, at that indefinably remote period when a third of mankind, among it the ancestors of nearly the whole present population of Europe, constituted as yet only one

G

horde; and it appears at once that among the Indo-Europeans fire was already then made, on the whole, in the same way as it has been in the present century in America and the South Sea Islands. The process by which the sacred fire in Hindostan is even now lighted consists in twirling, which, according to the description of eye-witnesses, perfectly resembles the churning of butter still practised there by milling the milk with a stirring-rod. According to Stevenson's description, one piece of wood is drilled into another by pulling a string tied to it with a jerk with the one hand while the other is slackened, and so alternately until the wood takes fire. The fire is received on cotton or flax by the bystanding Brahman. We shall be obliged to own that this mode of producing fire well suits the character of a period when man was not only destitute of any metal but even as yet of stone implements—that is to say, of a wood age, such as must have preceded the stone age. A more primitive process can hardly be presumed. But, neverthelesss, it is not simple, not obvious enough, to appear independently with such uniformity at several points of the earth. Though we do not know the way in which the fire-drill may have spread from India and Australia to South America, it can scarcely have been invented at various times in the same way. There are many puzzling though undeniable vestiges extant of a primeval connection between Eastern Asia and Mexico. As regards the Australian Archipelago, the influence of India on it is clearly to be proved by linguistic elements and legends. Nay,

there is a chain of traditions and borrowings that ex-
tends over those islands as far as Madagascar and
Central Africa; and we meet again among the Kaffres
and negro tribes with fables and tales which can have
reached them by no other way, and which may be a
hint to us not to decide too hastily to what distances
the influence man exercises on man may extend. Once
discovered in one place, fire could not but be diffused
by immigrants from more gifted tribes among those
inferior to them, and soon carried over the whole earth.
The contagious power of ideas is, in fact, greater in
primitive times, and the isolation of peoples less, than
is frequently believed. Together with the great diver-
gences of contemporaneous stages of culture, there has
been at all times going on among the entire human
race a reciprocal action, which would not allow too
violent contrasts to exist together for too long a space
without their being adjusted. As in modern times
firearms have incessantly spread, so a much more important transformation of the outward life of prehistoric
times could not possibly escape being gradually carried
from one dwelling-place to another, and sooner or later
the wonderful spectacle of a nocturnal camp-fire would
call forth a universal imitation even in the remotest
corners of the inhabited world, though it should
have had to penetrate from the one hemisphere to
the other by way of the Polar region, where Greenlanders and Eskimos form the connecting link.
But in realising the condition of the human race,
which, no doubt, lies far behind us, and has, therefore,

something strange to our conceptions—the condition, I say, in which mankind were when, on the whole, they lived as yet without fire, and had first to become acquainted with it as a new invention on the part of a favoured tribe—it will at least not appear incredible to us that with the use of fire the mode of producing it, the primitive fire apparatus of the earliest times, were simultaneously diffused.

While so many uncivilised tribes of the present time, by their having preserved the fire-drill in daily use, afford us a living view of a primitive condition, the holy use which Brahmans make of it may throw a light upon the history of that important implement. In the age when the earliest Veda hymns took their origin, the sacred fire was daily lighted in the early morning by the priests. With the greatest solicitude they attended to the prescribed measures of two equally sized pieces of wood, of the spindle which, proceeding from the one, was fixed on to the other, and the cord which served for the turning; nay, even the choice of the wood was not a matter of indifference; it was chiefly to be composed of the açvattha or banana tree, the so-called *Ficus religiosa*. Among the Romans, the vestal flame, when gone out, was, as Plutarch relates, rekindled by means of a species of primitive reflector by the sunlight, but, according to other reports, by drilling, for which the priests had to make use of the wood of a fruit-tree. It is most remarkable that we should meet with quite a corresponding practice among the Peruvians: there, too, the sacred fire in-

trusted to the sun-virgins was, when by' mistake' or·
accidentally extinguished, relighted either by the sun
by means of a golden concave mirror, or by rubbing
together two pieces of wood. Among the Iroquois the
fire in the huts is extinguished every year, and relighted
by the magician with the flint or by the friction of two
pieces of wood. The Mexicans celebrated every fifty-
two years a great fire-festivity, or a regeneration of the
world, the doom of which they dreaded at the end of
each such period. All fires were then extinguished; a
grand procession of men, disguised in the garb of the
gods, repaired, accompanied by an immense crowd, to
Mount Huichashta, and here, at midnight, the fire was
reproduced by two pieces of wood being rubbed together
on the chest of the prisoner of war intended for the
sacrifice. Amidst shouts of joy raised by the people,
who were looking on in eager expectation from all the
hills, temples, and roofs round about, the flame blazed
forth from the stake of the victim, and was thence
spread before daybreak over all the altars and hearths of
Anahuac. And if we return from this distant region to
our own immediate neighbourhood, we have even here
numerous, certainly more innocent, traces of a production of fire in the same primitive fashion originally
adopted for religious purposes. In various parts of
Germany, as well as in England, Scotland, and Sweden,
the practice continued down to the very latest centuries
of lighting the so-called need-fire, on certain days of
the year, by turning a wooden windlass bored into a
stake, and keeping it in motion by a rope wound round it.
·From almost everywhere reports have reached us that

all the fires in houses had first to be extinguished and renewed again by this need-fire, endowed, as it was supposed to be, with a variety of miraculous virtues.

If one could doubt the omnipotent, irresistible progress of human thought over unmeasured space, this truly astounding agreement of German customs with those of the aborigines of America, this religious renewal of fire common to them both, would, I opine, alone suffice to rouse in us the belief in an unceasing intercommunication between all peoples, in a constant universal intercourse between all parts of the earth.

But, I would ask, what may have induced the ancient peoples to apply the art of fire-making in such universal agreement, to an extent embracing nearly the whole world, to purposes of divine worship? There is scarcely one people of antiquity in whose worship fire was not of quite a paramount importance. Among the Persians its sacredness is so evident as to have made their religion be for a long time regarded as absolute fire-worship. But fire was here, as everywhere else, only a type, a representation of the heavenly fire, *i.e.*, the sun. Comparative mythology has taught us that the earliest divinities of the Indo-European peoples were gods of light, and no one doubts that the sun occupied the highest place among them. We are less certain, however, as to the conceptions of Nature which lie hidden beneath the charming veil of primitive metaphors and legends, or as to the meaning of the infinitely entangled magic knot of struggles, adventures, and miracles, and that world of odd shapes of partly sublime, partly strangely repulsive appearance, that world of gods, demons, giants, dwarfs, and monsters of every description with which their mythology abounds.

It is, however, indisputable that the struggle between light and darkness—the sun combating and vanquishing the powers of darkness—is the central idea of all those contrasts with which the inexhaustible imagination of man sports, ever again creating new shapes, and on which for centuries all the ingenuity of the human mind was exclusively employed. Professor Adalbert Kuhn is of opinion that the sacred fire was even in later times lighted by drilling only from adherence to ancient custom. But there is no testimony extant that primitive times knew of a profane, over and above the sacred fire-making apparatus, and from all the facts transmitted to us I have gained a firm conviction that men, far from transferring the use of the fire-drill from daily life into divine worship, invented it, on the contrary, precisely for the purpose of such worship, and only subsequently learned to use it in practical life. Aye! I cannot forbear declaring that fire is a religious discovery: it sprang from the worship of deities in times when men, on the one hand, did not yet even feel a practical want of producing it, and were, on the other, not yet even capable at all of reflecting on a technical invention such as fire-making by friction.

In the Veda hymns, that purest expression of the childlike faith of man, we see the divinities of heaven, the sun and dawn, unceasingly extolled. Heaven and earth, conceived as living beings, as was the original conception of all peoples, are invoked in the early morning; often heaven as father, the earth as mother.

" Which," we read in one of these primitive hymns,
" which of the two arose sooner, which later, how they
originated, sages, who knoweth it ?   By their own
strength they bear the universe, like two wheels do
day and night revolve."   " Powerfully separating two
wheels," we read in another passage, " with the axle,
as it were, Indra fasteneth heaven and earth."   When
Ushas, dawn, arose, she was welcomed with songs by
the host of the pious worshippers who had awaited
her appearance with holy eagerness.   " She is approaching, she shineth forth, heaven's daughter, visible
now.   She, the mighty one, thrusteth out darkness by
light, and the glorious one produceth brightness."

In transparent metaphors the goddess of dawn is
celebrated, how she supersedes her black sister, night,
and precedes the sun-god.

" Heaven's daughter, lo ! hath appeared, dawning,
young, in reddish garment; mistress of every earth-
born blessing, Ushas, break forth, beneficent one,
here now this day !   She followeth in the wake of
her who preceded: she goeth before the everlasting
ones who are coming ; dawning, she calleth forth all
that liveth, and whatever is dead Ushas awakeneth.
When will she be united to those who have shone
already and will yet be shining ?   She followeth her
predecessors with eagerness ; united to others, lus-
trously she leadeth the way.   Gone are they, the mortals
who once beheld the breaking of former dawns ; now
she is here and is seen by us, and others will come
who one day shall behold her. . . . Ever before the
goddess dawned, and thus too the gracious one hath

dawned this day; and thus, too, she will dawn in later days, not aging, she, the immortal one, cometh to the sacrifice. In colours she shineth on the borders of heaven; the goddess strippeth off her black cover, awakening, Ushas with her red steeds, driveth on a beautifully appointed chariot. She carrieth gifts along with her, rich in blessings, and gaineth brightness in making her appearance. Ushas gloweth, the last of those that have passed, and the first of those that shine forth."

With such hymns the dawn was hailed 3000 years ago on the banks of the Indus. The seers of those days have long since passed away, and other mortals have come to behold immortal dawn. Although she no longer finds her ancient sacrifices amongst us, her sacred songs are still read by us after such a long interval, and those magic verses, of whose enchanting sounds I have only been able to present to you a faint echo, well deserve that, absorbed in the study of them, we watch for the dawn of day as did the primeval Hindoo poets who sang them.

Now, with these descriptions of the morning sky are blended those of the flames of the sacrificial fire, which was lighted daily in the early morning while it was still dark, and on account of its unfailing return is almost regarded as an independent phenomenon of Nature, and even celebrated as the god of fire, Agni, himself.

"Agni is awake," we read; "out of the earth riseth the sun-god; Ushas, the high yellow one, hath dawned."

"Up rose the red heaven-touching smoke; the men light Agni."

Other passages run thus: " By the might and greatness of the kindled blaze, heaven and earth alike in lustre shine. Up rise thy flames, the not old ones, Agni, the new-born, lighted. A red smoke thou ascendest heavenward, as a messenger thou goest, Agni, to the gods. Roused is Agni by men's lighting before Ushas, approaching like a cow. Like swarms flying up from the bough, his flames blaze forth towards heaven."

Amidst such hymns fire was made at the primeval seat of the progenitors of the Hindoo people. Often Agni is designated as the child of heaven and earth, but occasionally also as the child of the two pieces of wood; and, say the songs, scarcely born, the terrible child consumeth both his parents. This is no contradiction. The two pieces of wood are, indeed, heaven and earth. The revolution of heaven and earth produces the sun; by the turning of the sticks of wood, fire, his representative on earth, is produced. Hence precisely those gods to whom, in some Hindoo tradition, a golden fire-making apparatus is attributed, are the two horse-gods whom Max Müller has shown to refer to dawn. According to a Homeric hymn, the god who first used the fire-making apparatus was Hermes, also a god of dawn, a medium between the upper and lower world, and, like the Hindoo fire-god, a messenger of the gods. Hence, too, the Hindoos do not choose the wood which is practically the fittest, but that of the *Ficus religiosa,* and that not only because this tree bears a reddish fruit, but, as is expressly said, and as analogies of other holy trees amongst kindred peoples, *e.g.,* the mistletoe, so sacred among the Gauls, testify, because it takes root upon other trees, and its branches hang down in great abundance. It is manifestly a type of the sun, for he is often compared to a wonderful tree, whose roots are high up in the air, and which sends down its rays like branches on to the earth.

Of some remarkable Teutonic customs, preserved down to modern times from the remotest antiquity, the signification is almost unmistakable. In many parts of the "*Mark*" (Brandenburg) the need-fire is lighted in the nave of a wheel by drilling. The same is reported from the last century of the Isle of Mull on the west coast of Scotland, and is found again in the Frisian laws. In many other parts of Germany and France they used to light instead, mostly in the night of the summer solstice, disks or wheels, then flung them up high so as to make them describe a shining curve in the air; or, as was still the practice at the Moselle a hundred years ago, a burning wheel was made to roll down from the top of a mountain into the river. It is surely nothing but the diurnal course of the sun which was intended to be symbolised by these ceremonies on some distinguished day of the year, and equally certain it is that the flame lighted every morning in prehistoric times by the Hindoos had the same object. When, full of expectation, the wise men of that period, at the dawn of the morning, directing their glances towards the East where the shining god was to appear to them, prefigured by twirling two pieces of wood, that most primitive type of the great progenitors of the two worlds revolving like a wheel, the revolution of the heavens which was preparing the advent of the beneficent appearance of the new-born day; when in their naïve faith they imagined they might assist or even further that revolution by this incessantly repeated holy work, and when in the centre of the small type of the world which they were turning between their hands the spark suddenly flashed up, as did up yonder in the great celestial world the wonderful majestic flame of the morning sun—what joy and awe must have thrilled their hearts on seeing that the great god of heaven, Agni himself, had descended into their sanctuaries, was sitting as a guest at their sacrifice, and as a priest himself bore it up in smoke to heaven! And if there ever was a time when the fire first burst forth from the match—the new, strange guest, exciting, perhaps, fear and dismay—it was a god who was to be approached and cultivated, and for whose sake men would venture what, for mere utility's sake, they would perhaps never have ventured, as men indeed have at all times suffered incredible things for their religious convictions' sake. That the fire was transferred from this holy origin into daily life, as, for instance, we find, at the Mexican fire-festival, the sacred fire spread over all the hearths, we shall deem less surprising when we consider to what extent fire was sacred still among the classical nations, and that it was regarded as holy not only on the altars, but on the domestic hearths. From the standpoint of our culture we find it hard to derive what is quite common from mythic, purely fantastic sources. But this may be proved by innumerable minor and greater instances extending over our whole cultural life. Tobacco-smoking sprang from the fire-worship of the Indian tribes; the umbrella from the parasol, which was originally a sacred type of the sun; gold owes its high value to its sunlike, and therefore sacred colour. In 1811 the captive Russian Captain Golownin was asked in Japan whether the Russians had changed their religion, Laxmann, who in 1792 had been there as ambassador, having worn a pigtail dusted with flour. So ingrained is the habit with non-Europeans of seeing a connection even between most insignificant customs and religion.

One more point remains to be touched upon, one objection to be removed which might be raised to the accidental discovery of fire by using the fire-making apparatus. Was not the ignition of the pieces of wood at the ceremonies we have described foreseen and intended? Are we to think that the turning process was originally purposeless? I am decidedly of opinion that that religious toying consisted essentially only in the rotatory motion without regard to what might become of it. This seems to me to result from the fact that the process of turning in order to obtain fire was not the only one that served the same purpose; the preparation of butter by a quite analogous process was likewise holy, and butter therefore a principal element in the morning sacrifice. Nay, even the mill, which in its simplest shape consisted of two stones and a twirling-rod, and therefore very much resembled that ancient fire-machine from which it has perhaps developed, is frequently brought in connection with sun-myths, and significant legends tell of mills which grind gold. But I must more particularly mention here a curious religious implement which, in the sphere where it occurs, has certainly lost the connection with its origin, and is not now understood, but may perhaps receive as well as spread light in the environment in which we are able to place it.

In the domain of Buddhism and its transformations, in Tibet among the Kalmuks and Mongols no less than in Japan, it has been observed with wondering that prayers are not only spoken but likewise offered up with equally great merit by a machine. Round a cylinder which is set in rotatory motion by a strap by means of a spring-wheel, slips of paper of great length, on which prayers are inscribed, unroll, repeating the same text in a hundred-fold and a thousand-fold copy, it being the more efficient for the salvation of the being for whom the prayer is offered up the more copies wind round the cylinder. And not by man's hand alone, but by pendulums too, by wind-sails, nay, quite like wheels through a millrace, the prayer-wheels are set in motion. There are prayer-mills containing the identical formula which was printed at Petersburgh for that purpose a hundred millions of times, and which, therefore, by being turned ten times, effect as much salvation as if the formula had been recited a thousand millions of times. It is, no doubt, not wholly unjustified that attention should have been directed to the progress which is to be expected even here from steam power, and to the rapidity with which an incredible quantity of salvation might be produced by steam-mills. We receive, indeed, the impression of something eminently heathen when we see people find merit and a salutary effect in such strictly mechanical practices, void of all sentiment of devoutness. But this mechanism evidently has its reasons notwithstanding. Buddhism is a comparatively modern and reflected religion, but its symbols are transformations, and in the last instance invariably proceed from rites practised in the earliest natureworship. Originally it was not the prayers but the turning of the wheel itself which wrought salvation. In Japan there are found in the cemeteries posts to which a simple iron wheel is attached that can be turned with the hand. The relation of the revolution of the wheel to salvation is rendered intelligible by the representation of the metempsychosis under this image. But even that is only a transformation of the primitive practices of milling and turning as symbols of the diurnal revolution of the sun and the firmament, exactly as is the habit of the Hindoo, by way of reverence, to circumambulate objects or persons with their faces turned to the right. At present men will inquire, if not into the purpose of acts and ceremonies, at least into their signification. But to the earliest acts of mankind this method of treating things is not quite applicable; their customs had no signification, they were not intended to express any ideas. They are not symbols but instinct. What in the twilight of primitive history we perceive of the mysterious doings of mankind shows us our own image singularly altered, aye! of almost ghastly strangeness. If by circumambulation, by circular processions or races, by turning objects of various kinds, the movement of the heavens is imitated, these are outbursts of a once powerful instinct, of an imitative impulse which must once have swayed mankind with irresistible might at a certain stage of their existence. The variety of games, dances, representations, and mummeries of the ancient peoples in honour of the gods, the lamentation over the effigy of the dead Adonis, the processions of the Egyptian priests in the guise of animal-gods, have some resemblance to children's games. But we see all this proceed with a solemn gravity which has in it something ghostly, as it were. A similar serious game of childlike mankind it was which gradually taught them the use of fire and the preparation of food, which at first was only a sacrificial viand; indeed, a history of sacrifices and religious ceremonies in general would perhaps comprise, among many other surprising facts, a history of the art of cooking too. Belief, legend, mythology are all only one, perhaps not even the fullest, aspect of religion. As the mimic instinct appearing everywhere in the history of religion reminds us of the beginnings of language, in which I can likewise see only the effects of an involuntary instinctive mimicry and imitation, so in the spell which fire has exercised over men another analogy to the original source of language is presented to us, in so far as here, too, it is proclaimed aloud that it is the eye to which we owe our being raised above brute nature. Not the beneficent effect of fire, not its usefulness, not even its grateful warmth it is which are extolled in the primitive monuments, but its lustre, its red glow; and in so far as the names given by language may be interpreted with certainty, it is likewise neither the warmth, nor even the quality of burning, consuming, or causing pain, but the red colour from which they proceed. The sense of colour, then, was the earliest interest which attracted men to the fire. In this purely human interest lies the solution of the riddle why man alone possesses fire, but, at the same time, we may on closer investigation divine also something of the immense importance which the development of this sense of colour had for mankind.

Though man undoubtedly struggled up to his present height from the poverty and helplessness of the animal, we still see his early childhood already clothed in the sheen of the ideal, and it is by no means necessity that made him inventive, nor his practical sense that prompted him to ameliorate his material condition, but precisely in his earliest productions inspiration and fancy appear most at work, and what was destined to become of the greatest benefit to him is not his capacity of discovering what is useful, but the artistic disposition in him which led him to shape and fashion without any definite object, and the sense of heavenly beauty, a ray of which fell on his eye.

To all appearance it was not at first the increase of comfort which endeared fire to man, nor the pleasure in more savoury food, still less its usefulness in industry, which indeed had not yet even dawned upon him. But it was the light in which he rejoiced. With it he had overcome the uncomfortable dread of the night, during which he was liable to all kinds of danger, and was helplessly abandoned to the attacks of the beasts of the forest issuing forth in quest of prey. We who illumine the night by flaming torches and radiant chandeliers, or electric light as bright as the sun, we can scarcely realise those horrors which man felt in the reign of darkness, which was unbroken as yet by any art, and populated his imagination with ghastly shapes. We can barely sympathise with that anxiety which still speaks so vividly in the prayers of the Veda poets, or with the terrors that for a long time seized the intimidated hearts of men on the occasion of solar eclipses, when they feared the sun's light might disappear for ever even in the day, and an everlasting night break in upon them. And yet how comparatively modern is the wax-candle, nay, the oil lamp! In Homer it is still shavings and a bundle of brushwood which illumined the spacious halls.

Wherever we cast our eye, a chain of development is shown in the history of every object, the possession of which at present seems to us quite a matter of course, and at a misty distance there looms a period when such development had not yet begun. It is true it is only an outward possession which we see disappear with fire, with artificial light, from the series of our earthly blessings, but still we are ever again reminded thereby of our remotest past, of the singularly wonderful fortune that has led our species up to be at the head of the animal world, and of this earth in general. A few steps backward and we should see a second blessing disappear from this precious inheritance of humanity, and then a third; religion too, and finally language. A retrospective glance at those remote times, such as our age affords above all its predecessors, liberates our soul by making it partake of a past infinity. When Goethe, absorbed in osteological studies, confessed to have meditated amidst world-stirring events his discovery of the physical affinity of man to brutes, Börne's anger was roused, his ardent spirit yearning impatiently for deeds. And when the July revolution broke out, and the faithful Eckermann, finding Goethe greatly excited on the subject of the great event that had happened at Paris, was about to begin to speak of the faults of the overthrown ministers, Goethe replied, " We do not seem to comprehend each other. I do not speak at all of those people; my mind is occupied with quite different things. I am speaking of the dispute that has openly broken out in the Academy between Cuvier and Geoffroy de St. Hilaire, of such paramount importance to science. Henceforth mind will rule in France too in the investigation of nature, and prevail over matter. Glimpses will be caught of great maxims of creation, of God's mysterious workshop. Now," continued Goethe, " Geoffroy de St. Hilaire too is decidedly on our side, and with him all his more distinguished disciples and adherents in France. This event is of incredible value to me, and I justly exult over the finally arrived universal triumph of a cause to which I have devoted my life, and which is pre-eminently my own." The idea the victory of which Goethe at that time saw with his mind's eye, and which Geoffroy de St. Hilaire declared to be his own—the idea of the evolution of the world—will, I doubt not, emancipate the world as much as any of the greatest historical achievements did. Nor do I fear being misconstrued when I own to you, my honoured fellow-towns-men and women, that the thought has often floated through my mind that the soil of this city of ours possesses some claim to this liberating idea of evolution; that in this town, which owes so much to natural development, the voice of admonition sounds doubly loud to continue to meditate the idea of the development of humanity, aye! perhaps to think it out to an end. This idea will one day teach us what man has to expect and to claim for himself from humanity and from nature. And as it opens to us a vista into the future, so with it begins to open a retrospective view of the past, just as happened with space from the moment when the sky ceased to arch over us as a stony cover, and we began to cast glances into, and indulge in speculations on, the unbounded universe. History is no longer a limited horizon; the same things are not in wearisome uniformity repeated from century to century, but in unfathomed depths one form of existence succeeds another. Nature reveals to us her wonders in an infinite series, and the soul of man is elevated, becoming a heavenly genius which soars with mighty wing through eternity.

On the Primitive Home of the Indo-Europeans.

THE discovery of the primitive stock of the Indo-
Europeans, which has been made within the past
sixty years, is a fact of incredible importance, and
of incalculable influence on the conception of man's
earliest past. The almost marvellous results which
our century has obtained in the decipherment of the
hieroglyphics and cuneiform inscriptions led to a direct
knowledge, gained from the monuments themselves, of
the life of peoples which one could not till then have
hoped ever to see resuscitated from its millennial sleep.
Historical details have been authenticated, dating from
times which fancy had ever regarded as its indisputable
domain and had populated with grotesque shapes. But
the people of the pyramids and hieroglyphics is, notwithstanding, an historical, well-known, palpable people.
It is certainly astounding that we should have learned
to find some centuries before Moses—that earliest histo-
rian, as the last century was fond of calling him—the
names of Palestinian cities—*e.g.*, of the still existing
Zephath—on Egyptian monuments. We are strangely
moved and feel a thrill of awe running through us, as

on entering a mysterious sanctuary, when we see before our eyes the veil lifted from the deeply-hidden
and dark past.   But such more especially are our
emotions when we approach the primitive stock from
which the head and flower of the whole human race
was destined to proceed—the stock from which has
sprung the present civilised Europe with its mighty
colonies, and not less so a large portion of the population
of Asia, as far as the boundaries of China.   We have
here, in this people in its primitive condition, a germ
before us with an abundance of developments latent
within it, as it were ; and though history does not contain any record of this people, and it has not left any
monuments itself, so that we are able only to infer its
existence, yet we can by no means doubt its having
existed.   How did a people in such a primitive condition live ?   How did it think ? how speak ?   These
questions alone have a deep interest; but to them
must be added that all the civilisation of Europe, and,
more or less, the condition of mankind at the present
time, have been connected with the fortunes of that
primitive people and swayed by its intellectual capa-
cities, thus pointing back to the origin of that people
for their own.

On its being first remarked that in the languages
of Hindostan and Persia words and forms of words
occur bearing a striking resemblance to Latin, Greek,
and German words, many endeavoured to account for
this singular phenomenon by a mutual intercourse,
which they supposed to have carried foreign words

from one people to another. The Germans have borrowed their *marsch* (march) from the French; *halt*
(stop), which we must presume to be a more German
notion, was given to the French in exchange for it;
and *pascholl* is even Russian. Now it is no doubt
somewhat farther from Benares or Pondicherry to
Frankfort or Augsburg, and no 1813 probably ever
brought Germans and Hindoos together in a battle
of nations. Nevertheless—but I will let Adelung
speak here, because it is not uninteresting to see how
a man of considerable linguistic knowledge and much
judgment could, in 1806, still think on such questions.
"That even German elements should be found in
Persian has excited wonder, in some even astonishment. The fact is undeniable; and this German so
found in Persian does not consist only in a considerable
number of radical sounds and words, but also in derivative syllables and even grammatical forms. . . . This
phenomenon may be accounted for in two ways: either
by a subsequent intermixture after the two languages
were already formed, or by a common descent from
a more ancient mother tongue. The situation and
history of Persia seem to favour the former view.
Being situated on the way which nearly all the
savage hordes from Upper Central Asia had to take
to the West, it could not well continue wholly free
from an admixture with other conquering and con-
quered peoples. It is more especially known that
the Goths dwelt for several centuries by the Black,
and Caspian Seas—*i.e.*, at the gates of Persia; that,

with their savage bravery, they weighed down on
their neighbours, at the same time constantly trying
to push forward into more favoured countries. History
even mentions an entire Gothic tribe which had in-
vaded Persia and became amalgamated with the ancient
inhabitants into one people. Such may have been the
case with several tribes, especially when the Goths had
to give way to the Huns, though the meagre history of
those times does not record anything of it (Mithridates,
i. 277)." But now it is well known that the greatest difficulty encountered by such hypotheses was the great
number, and especially the sphere of ideas, of the words
which those Asiatic languages had in common with the
European ones. Who could believe that Persians and
Germans would just happen to have borrowed from
each other such words as *padar* = *Vater* (father), *madar*
= *Mutter* (mother), *biradar* = *Bruder* (brother), *ast* =
ist (is)? Hence even Adelung already inclined to the
second view—the descent from a common mothertongue. "The Parsee, Zend, and Pehlevî," he says, "are
very ancient languages, and near the seat of the first
formation of language, and may therefore descend, like
Sanskrit, if not from the first language itself, at least
from one of her oldest daughters. The Teutons, like
all ancient Western peoples, are descended from Asia,
and although we are now no longer able to determine
the region they inhabited previous to their emigration,
there are no reasons why we should not be allowed to
place them in Central Asia, bordering directly upon
Persia and Tibet, whose unsettled hordes have both

populated Europe and shaken it on more than one occasion." People then believed in a primitive language—the language of the first human beings—and looked for remnants of it in all languages. Thus the great agreement between two such "old" languages as German and Sanskrit was thought to be based on the preservation of a particularly great number of remnants of the "first language," or on the descent from "one of her oldest daughters." Immediately behind this separation of languages lay the building of the tower of Babel and Paradise. The conceptions of the origin of man and of that of the formation of the individual Indo-Teutonic peoples coalesced in the imagination.

It was Friedrich Schlegel who, in his brilliant work, "Ueber die Sprache und Weisheit der Indier" ("On the Language and Wisdom of the Hindoos," 1808), put an end to this want of clearness. He determined pretty accurately the limits comprising the Indo-European languages, and pronounced the Latin, Greek, Teutonic, and Persian, on the one hand, and the Armenian, Slavonic, and Keltic languages, on the other, to be, the former more nearly, the latter more remotely, related to Sanskrit. Other families of languages, *e.g.*, that to which Hebrew belongs, he decidedly excluded from this affinity. The relation of Sanskrit to the other cognate dialects he conceived as that of a mothertongue to its offsprings. Nay, taking his stand on the great agreement he also found in the sphere of the ideas and legends of India and the rest of antiquity, he declared the populations of Europe to be actual "Indian colonies," of which he makes the priests the special leaders, and held those colonies to have been more important and efficacious than, though not essentially different from, the later Greek settlements. Since then we have learned to recognise that such an analogy to an ordinary emigration, such as occurs in historic times, is not applicable to that primeval age. The European languages, Latin and German, for instance, do not bear to Sanskrit the relation of daughters, such as Spanish, Italian, and French do to Latin. Sanskrit, on the contrary, is only a co-ordinate sister-language, e.g., of German and Greek. Sanskrit and Greek bear the same relation to each other as French and Italian. The primary language, which should bear the same relation to the principal Indo-European languages as does Latin to her daughters, if such ever existed, is, at any rate, no longer extant. The dialect which the ancestors of the Teutons, Greeks, and Hindoos once spoke in common was no more Hindoo than German or Greek: it was the primitive Indo-European language. Hence, too, it was not the Hindoo people which all those ancestors together constituted, but the primitive *Indo-European people*. Besides, the earliest Indian literature still affords traces of the Hindoos having only by gradually advancing towards the east and the south reached the Ganges; they must have separated from their near relations, the Persians, at a comparatively late date only, in order to take possession of India proper. All the less did the primitive Indo-European people inhabit India. But where then did they dwell ? Which was the first home of the Indo-Europeans, who were destined to play so prominent and unique a part in history, and are at present spread over the whole earth, actually ruling it ? That with the earliest guesses at the kinship of European and Asiatic peoples the presumption was associated that the cradle of the Europeans had been Asia, may be gathered from what I have stated. Previously to my continuing to trace the history of the opinions on this question, permit me briefly to express my own present conviction, that the primitive home of the Indo-Europeans is to be looked for in Germany, perhaps more especially in its central and western parts.

The first to oppose the hypothesis, which is universally accepted though it has never been supported by evidence, of the descent of the Indo-Europeans from Asia was R. G. Latham. His opinion, as far as I am aware, is for the first time expressed in his work, " The Native Races of the Russian Empire " (London, 1854). In a subsequent work, "Elements of Comparative Philology " (London, 1862, p. 611), he establishes it in the following words :—

" Has the Sanskrit reached India from Europe, or have the Lithuanic, the Slavonic, the Latin, the Greek, and the German reached Europe from India ? If historical evidence be wanting, the *à priori* presumptions must be considered.

" I submit that history *is* silent, and that the presumptions are in favour of the smaller class having been deduced from the area of the larger rather than *vice versâ*. If so, the *situs* of the Sanskrit is on the eastern, or south-eastern, frontier of the Lithuanic; and its origin is European. . . .

"I do not deny the fact, as it is usually stated, as a fact. It may be one, in spite of any amount of presumptions against it. If sufficient evidence be brought forward in favour of it, I am prepared to take it as it is given. . . .

"I may be wrong, however, in asserting the absolute non-existence of evidence; in other words, in holding that the presumptions are, really, all we have to go on. Upon this I am open to correction. I can, however, truly say that, if there be evidence on the matter, I have failed, after a careful search, to find it. What I have found in its stead is a tacit assumption that, as the East is the probable quarter in which either the human species, or the greater part of our civilisation, originated, everything came from it. But surely, in this, there is a confusion between the primary diffusion of mankind over the world at large and those secondary movements by which, according to even the ordinary hypothesis, the Lithuanic, &c., came from Asia into Europe. . . . In zoology and botany the species is always deduced from the area of the genus, rather than the genus from the area of the species; and this is the rule which I go upon here. . . .

"The fact of a language being not only projected, so to say, into another region, but entirely lost in its own, is anything but unique. There is no English in Ger-

many. A better example, however, is found in the
Magyar of Hungary, of which no trace is to be found
within some 700 miles of its present area. Yet the
Magyar is not twelve hundred years old in Europe."

We shall see that not only is the evidence in favour
of the still accepted Asiatic hypothesis wanting, but
that the opposite assumption will, by a whole series of
arguments, be rendered highly probable; and, having
ascertained a sharply defined original European home
of the Indo-Europeans, we shall be enabled to establish
the latter hypothesis on a safe basis. ,

These arguments are of various descriptions. I shall
begin with a physiological phenomenon, which, though
certainly not decisive, yet, when considered in connection with other aspects of the question, is most noteworthy. The remarkable fair type, the combination
of light hair and blue eyes, are essentially confined to
Indo-European peoples. In the North, neighbouring
Fin tribes in some measure partake of this pecu-
liarity; with this exception, it is not met with any-
where. In the South it disappears, in some parts more,
in others less, even among the Indo-Europeans. How
are we to account for this circumstance? If the hair
and eyes of the Hindoos have become black, and even
the colour of their skin yellowish, this fact can hardly
be accounted for in any other way than by an intermixture with the aborigines of India. Something
similar is at least possible wherever we meet with
dark Indo-Europeans. But since, so far as we are
aware, no non-Indo-European people ever existed from

which the Northern Indo-Europeans could have con-
tracted the light colour, we are, from the ethnological
point of view, certainly more justified in regarding
the fair type, wherever we meet with it, as the un-
alloyed Indo-European type. This view favours the
assumption that the Indo-Europeans have remained
most unmixed where the blonde type shows itself
purest; and it is well known how much the latter
struck the Romans on their meeting with the Germans.
We shall, therefore, scarcely assume too much when
we claim the highest probability of indigenousness for
that people which has preserved the original type in
its greatest purity, and has least come into contact
with tribes foreign to its stock.

On an Egyptian monument, dating so far back as
the fourteenth century before Christ, there is to be
seen in a grouping of various races of men consisting of
Egyptians, Negroes, and Semites, also a representation, of masterly fidelity, of a man having a thoroughly
white skin, blue eyes, and blonde hair. Champollion
already recognised a European in this surprising
picture. That the Egyptians should, at so early a
period, have known of such men is most remarkable.
What people they may have belonged to we shall
perhaps discuss in the sequel; to meet premature
objections, however, let me observe that these men,
wherever may have been their home, and however far
they may have migrated from it, can nevertheless not
prove anything as regards the so much earlier period
that preceded the Indo-European migration. For

another monument of the eighteenth century B.C., where
an ape is designated by an Indian, or at least Aryan
name, *kaf* (Sanskrit, *kapi*), proves that the Indo-
Europeans must at all events have migrated to Asia
previously to that time. The Chinese, too, must very
early have known blonde-haired men, for "the black-
haired people" is an appellation of honour which the
ancient hymns of the Shi-King already bestow on them.
For one of the hymns in this collection, and evidently
not one of the oldest, we have an astronomical date,
viz., the year 777 before the Christian era.

Important data to aid us in deciding on the original
home of the Indo-Europeans lie in the inferences which
may be drawn from the sphere of words and ideas of the
Indo-European tribes. Since Professor Adalbert Kuhn
commenced, from an examination of the vocabulary
common to the cognate tribes, to draw conclusions as
to the stage of culture of the primitive people, our
conceptions of the mode of life of the peoples of that
period have daily assumed a more definite shape. Little
justified as Schlegel was in attributing the culture of an
individual historically known people to a primitive age
as well, yet it would be a great mistake to imagine the
condition of the prehistoric Indo-Europeans to have
been a species of embryonic existence or of semi-human
savageness. The primitive people was doubtless extremely barbarous, but it possessed a political organisa-
tion, bred cattle, carried on agriculture and even trade,
and had productions of skill and industry exhibiting a
comparatively high stage of culture, and a not incon-

siderable intercourse with other peoples. In other words, it was a real nation, more highly civilised than many existing out of Europe at this day. When we find the word *naus*, "ship," quite uniform, both in Greek and Sanskrit, and as an equivalent in Latin *navis*, in German *Naue*, *Nachen* (boat), there can be no doubt that this community of name must have its cause in the community of the object, and the possession of the ship must have preceded the separation of the languages here mentioned. But in the same way *Wagen* (waggon), *Rad* or *Welle* (wheel), *Achse* (axle), and *Joch* (yoke, harness), are likewise met with as far as India. The ancient Indo-Europeans, therefore, did not only go by boat, as the so-called savages likewise do, but they availed themselves besides of cars and waggons drawn by animals, a proceeding which indicates by no means a condition without reflection. Very abundant, ably treated materials, enabling us to judge of the life of the Indo-Europeans, are afforded us by Adolphe Pictet in his work "Les Origines Indo-Européennes" (Paris, i. partie 1859, ii. partie 1863), where nature and human life, such as they are exhibited in the vocabularies of the Indo-European languages, are described with great completeness. Certainly too much may be inferred from the possession of a word. Thus, *e.g.*, from the uniformity with which the name of the *Hund* (hound, dog) occurs in all the Indo-European dialects, the possession of this domestic animal has been inferred; whereas it is more than probable that in the prehistoric times the dog was still wild, and known to the Indo-.

Europeans only in the untamed condition. A still graver and yet rather general error will easily become comprehensible on considering the mode in which the separation of the peoples must have come to pass. The once undivided nucleus of so many nations can certainly not be assumed to have at some time or other burst asunder in all directions at once, so as in this way to form the present nations that have sprung from it. The separation must have taken place at various times and successively. The actual affinity existing between the various languages places this proposition beyond all doubt. Sanskrit and ancient Persian or Zend, *e.g.*, are so much more closely related than, say, Sanskrit and Latin, that, as no one doubts, the Persians must necessarily have a special affinity to the Hindoos, which may be accounted for by the circumstance that the separation of these two nations is not yet so very old, not so old by a long way as that of the Romans and Hindoos. Between the Lithuanic and the Slavonic there exists a similar special affinity. It may be easily perceived how premature it would be to consider a word found only in Persián and Sanskrit as a primitive possession of the Indo-Europeans, and of such an error no linguist will be likely to render himself guilty. But as long as of some other peoples the succession in which they have separated from the original stock is not yet accurately ascertained, the danger of similar fallacies is very great. Thus, for instance, Benfey (in his Preface to Fick's "Wörterbuch der Indogermanischen Grundsprache" ("Dictionary of the Original Indo-Germanic

I

Language "), in describing the high stage of culture which the ancient Indo-Europeans must have reached, says, "They had weapons, especially arrows; they painted and composed poetry, especially hymns." The word on which the inference respecting arrows is based can be none other than the Greek *ios*, "arrow," which is nearly related to the Sanskrit *ischus*. But if arrows were certainly known to the Greeks and Hindoos at the time when they were still united, does it follow hence that they must have been known to the actual primitive people which, among others, comprised the ancestors of the Teutons as well? It is, indeed, for many reasons very probable that the Greeks, though not so nearly related to the Indians and Persians as these are to each other, are yet pre-eminently so, and must have been longer united with them than the Teutonic and Gallic, probably even than the Italic tribes. Now in none of the languages which, accordingly, are more distantly related to Sanskrit than is the Greek language, is there a word for "arrow" comparable to the word *ischus* to be met with; on the contrary, each branch of the Indo-European family uses a special word for "arrow" as well as for "bow." The Romans, *e.g.*, say for bow and arrow, *arcus* and *sagitta;* the Russians, *luk* and *stryela;* while for sword, *e.g.*, there is found among the Hindoos *asis*, and among the Romans *ensis, i.e.,* a common appellation. We must, therefore, conversely conclude that the primitive Indo-European people did *not* know the bow. Our word *Bogen* (bow) signified in the earliest times the bow of the arm, the elbow

(Sanskrit, *báhus;* Greek, *péchys*).　As to the painting of the Indo-Europeans, we shall soon return to it. These observations likewise apply to the hymns.　However great the probability that the people in question may not have been wholly destitute of hymns, we have no linguistic evidence of it: for a similar reason, *hymnos,* of which Benfey thinks, proves nothing.

As is evident, therefore, it is necessary somewhat to modify our conception of the primitive Indo-European people.　We must, in fact, not think of one such, but of several succeeding each other in strata.　One of the latest strata is represented by the time when Indians and Persians still formed one people, and which may be called the *Aryan* period.　An older stratum shows us the time when the Aryan people was united with the Greeks.　Let us call this the *Aryo-Hellenic* period. A good deal of what has been thought to belong to the Indo-Europeans collectively is merely Aryo-Hellenic. The Aryo-Hellenes were a highly cultivated people in a quite different sense from the Indo-Europeans.　They had real, doubtless sacerdotal, poetry in well-developed regular metres.　As regards that period, we shall yet one day succeed in placing it in a clear, well-nigh historical light.

With the question as to the people, that as to its original seat likewise assumes a different aspect. After abandoning the Indian hypothesis, the Aryan region, the home of the still undivided Hindoos and Persians, the north-west of India was assumed to be the cradle of all the Indo-Europeans.　From here the

kindred peoples, one after another, must have migrated.
Hindoos and Iranians, with their numerous rami-
fications, remained behind last, and finally separated,
the former migrating eastwards, the latter westwards.
Latham presupposes an Indo-European population in
Europe, to which the Indians likewise once belonged.
He endeavours to determine the seats which the Indians
occupied on European soil, and assumes, by way of
hypothesis, Podolia or Volhynia to have been such,
guided in this assumption by a certainly one-sided
conception of a specially close relationship between
Sanskrit and Lithuanic. Benfey very appropriately
adduces for a primeval European home the absence of
a community of names for the specially Asiatic animals,
such as the tiger and the camel, for instance. Pictet, in
his excellent work above quoted, had already employed
the same method, and attempted, from an abundant
stock of like and unlike designations of natural objects,
to conclude to the country to which the objects named
by an identical or similar word refer. Thus, for instance, from the manifest identity of Slavonic, Latin,
and German words for *Meer* (ocean, sea) among each
other and with the Sanskrit *mîra* (ocean), he, equally
with Benfey, infers that the Indo-Europeans of primitive times must have known some sea. He takes it to
be the Caspian, and places the original home of the
Indo-Europeans in Bactria and the valley of the Oxus.

If we consider that the Aryo-Hellenes may have
become isolated by their own migration, as well as by
the emigration of their brethren, and bear in mind that

for this very reason the abode of the Aryo-Hellenes, previous to the formation of a separate Greek people, need not have been the primitive seat of the Indo-Europeans, we shall have to deal with the materials from which linguistic inferences are to be drawn touching the original home of the Indo-Europeans, in the same way as with the inferences concerning their stage of culture and mode of life. · Peoples and languages do not originate by fits and starts, nor are the migrations which have created the chief branches of the Indo-European world of peoples to be understood as sudden, fitful, or violent breakings up. In a great many instances the spreading doubtless goes on gradually, and equally so does the estrangement, and with it the marked linguistic divergence. Hence the first starting-point of the whole movement is perhaps more easily to be discovered than are the intermediate stages. Now for this first starting-point or the original home of the Indo-Europeans we have a tolerably good guide in the *tree vegetation*, such as it is exhibited in languages which have been separated so long as German and Sanskrit or German and Greek. Here three trees especially are prominent, which must have received their names at one and the same time, and must therefore have been found together in the region where they were named, viz., the *birch*, the *beech*, and the *oak*.

The *birch*, as is well known, is that tree whose name recurs with the most decided uniformity in India and the greater part of Europe. It is called in Sanskrit

bhûrdschas, in Lithuanic *beržas*, in Russian *bereza*.
The Lithuanic *ž* sounds like a French *j ;* in the Russian word, which, through Berezina, *i.e.*, birchwood, has
acquired so terrible a celebrity, *z* is pronounced like in
French as a soft *s*. We can account for the slightest
phonetic divergence by which this name is distinguished from our *Birke* (birch). The ancient Indo-
European form must have been *bhĕrgás*. The short *ĕ*
is an unaccented, vaguely pronounced vowel, which in
German developed into *i*, in Sanskrit into *u*. In a
still earlier time the word doubtless sounded *bhargas*.
The permutation of the original *g* into a German *k*
ensued legitimately according to Grimm's law; the
transitions into *dsch* in Sanskrit and into soft *s* in
Russian are not more striking than is, for instance,
the pronunciation of *Cyrus* (Italian *Ciro*, " *Tchiro*,"
French *Cyrus*) for *Kurush*. That the *bh* had to be
transmuted in German, Lithuanic, and Russian into *b*
is also quite according to rule.

What did the name of the birch signify for the ancient Indo-Europeans ? The conception which may
have guided so early a time in naming trees is in itself
decidedly interesting, and in this instance the nomenclature has an additional and quite peculiar interest.
Grimm declines to explain the word birch. He says " the
root is entirely hidden in the dark." Pictet assumes
an affinity to *Borke* (bark), and this explanation is
no doubt very satisfactory as a matter of fact, for
birch-bark was already at an early age used in many
ways, among others, in India, as Pictet himself men-

tions, for writing purposes. Nevertheless I hold myself
bound to derive the name of the *Birke* (birch) from
its colour. The *Birkhuhn* (grouse or moorhen) is
usually conceived to be a fowl living in birch forests
and feeding on birch buds. But apart from the fact
that this is not the bird's only mode of life, and that
it is even found in the treeless steppes of Southern
Russia (whereat Kohl, misled by the name of the bird,
was not a little astonished), how are we in that case to
understand *Birkfuchs* (common fox)? But tree, bird,
and fox have plainly something in common. The
Birkfuchs is a fox with a white spot (*Blume;* cf. my
work just published, "Ursprung der Sprache" ["On
the Origin of Language"], page 243), as contradistin-
guished from a *Brandfuchs* (*Canis alopex*), which has a
black spot. The grouse has whitish spots, and so has
birch-bark. *Haselhuhn* (hazel-grouse), too, is generally derived from the hazel-nut tree. But the English *haze* means "grey," and doubtless not only hazel
means a grey plant, but even *Hase* (hare) means nothing
more and nothing less than the "grey one." Hence
perhaps, too, the *Haselmaus* (dormouse) is called so
from likewise being of ash-grey colour. The latter
analogy also favours the assumption that the syllable
Birk (birch) was not only intended to designate birch-
like hues, but that its primary meaning already was
white or spotted with light marks; and there is a root
admitting of ready comparison in the Sanskrit *bharg*,
German *breh* or *berh*, signifying light and light colour
(bright), and whence, too, *Bertha*, for instance, *i.e.*,

Berchta, the *bright* one, is derived. Accordingly, *Birke*
would imply " the white one," and the scientific appellation which the tree to this day bears, *Betula alba*,
would lie already in its primitive name. The *betula* is
called by Pliny a Gallic tree. In fact, the Keltic name
of the birch is *beith ;* and though diverging, it might
have been derived from the same primary form as
Birke, in which case *betula* would likewise already
signify *alba*. In support of this supposed primary
sense of "white," I can adduce the following additional
argument. The Romans, not wanting the name of the
birch for their native vegetation, made use of it in
another way. In *fraxinus*, the name of the *ash* (French
frêne), the affinity to birch has long since been recognised. Now the ash happens to have the whitish hue
in common with the birch. Nay, more, the word " ash "
(German *Esche*) itself likewise means " white." The
corresponding Russian word is *yaseny*, "ash," from *yasen*,
" clear." With this Russian word not only ash (old High
German *asc*), but probably too the Latin *ornus*, wild
ash, manna ash, in which the *r* may have originated in
s, is connected.

No one can fail to recognise the *Buche* (beech) in the
Latin *fagus*. In German, *u* has its origin in long *a*, as
in *Mutter* (mother), *Bruder* (brother), &c. *B* corresponds quite according to rule to the Latin *f*, and
German *ch* to the Latin *g*. Equally unmistakable is
the affinity of the Greek *phégos*. But—and this is a
much-discussed singularity—the Greek word does not
signify " beech," but a species of oak. The common

property which rendered it possible to employ a name of the beech for that of an oak has been supposed by some to be the eatableness of the fruit of each—the acorns of the one, and those of the other, called beech acorns—and accordingly they explained "beech" by the Greek *ephagon*, "I ate." For my own part, I am of opinion that we have here an instance analogous to the transfer of the name of the birch to the ash. It was the darker bark, as there the light one, which yielded the point of comparison. I appeal here, as I did above, to the *Buchmaus* or *Bilchmaus* (fat dormouse, *Mus glis*), or garden squirrel, to the *Buchfinken* (chaffinch), *i.e.*, redfinch, and to *Buchwaizen* (buckwheat), though these names admit of other explanations besides this, and would remind the reader of the Greek *phaios*, "grey." For the rest, the primary form of *Buche* (beech), which must have been *bhâga*, strikingly resembles that of *Birke* (birch), *bharga*, and this can scarcely be accidental when we consider that in Keltic too the beech is called *beath*, and the birch *beith*. In order to comprehend the considerable divergence of our modern High German forms, it has to be remembered that *rg*, as a rule, is converted in that dialect into *rk*, *e.g.*, the Greek *ergon* (originally *vergon*), German *Werk* (work); while in general *g* becomes *ch*, *e.g.*, *ego*, *ich* (I).[1] Now, is it not remarkable that not only

[1] The English form, "beech," strictly speaking, corresponds to our *Büche*. A word accurately corresponding to *Buche* would preserve the *k* in the same way as does "book," *Buch*. As here, so in birch too the vowel is the cause of the permutation of the *k* into *ch*, while, *e.g.*, the *Borke* is bark.

Esche (ash), but even *Eiche* (oak) should be formed quite in the same way? And as the *ch* in *Esche*, being a permutation of *g*, seems to be a mere derivative which is wanting in the Russian form of the word, may we not conclude that in *Buche*, *Birke*, and *Eiche*, too, *bha*, *bhar*, and *ai* only form the roots? For this reason I also surmise that the origin of those names of the trees belongs to one and the same period, such being generally the case with words formed according to quite the same rule. The root *ai*, too, which, after the deduction of the formative syllable, would be left of *Eiche*, seems to imply a colour, viz., *black*. In Greek we meet with the name *aigilops* for a species of oak; another name of a tree is *krataigos*; finally, *aigeiros* is the black poplar. In Lithuanic the oak is called *aźolas*, *auźolas*, or *uźolas*. I have elsewhere endeavoured to render it probable that the syllable *Ei* in *Eisen* (iron), too, signifies black, and is connected with a Sanskrit adjective meaning "coloured."

What may have made the Greeks transfer the name of the beech to the oak? This question has led Professor Max Müller to very ingenious though extremely hazardous conjectures. He first draws attention to a similar transfer of the name of our *Föhre* (fir), comparing it with the Latin *quercus* (oak). Let us hear the illustrious linguist himself on the subject.

"At first sight," he says, "the English word *fir* does not look very like the Latin *quercus*, yet it is the same word. If we trace *fir* back to Anglo-Saxon, we find it there under the form of *furh*. According to Grimm's law, *f* points to *p, h* to *k;* so that in Latin we should have to look for a word the consonantal skeleton of which might be represented as *prc.* Guttural and labial tenues change, and as Anglo-Saxon *fîf* points to *quinque*, so *furh* leads to Latin *quercus*, 'oak.' In old High German, *foraha* is *Pinus silvestris ;* in modern German, *Föhre* has the same meaning. But in a passage quoted from the Lombard laws of Rothar, *fereha*, evidently the same word, is mentioned as a name of oak (roborem aut quercum quod est *fereha*); and Grimm in his 'Dictionary of the German Language' gives *ferch* in the sense of oak, blood, life.

"It would be easy enough to account for a change of meaning from fir, or oak, or beech to tree in general, or *vice versâ*. We find the Sanskrit *dru*, 'wood' (cf. *druma*, 'tree,' *dâru*, 'log'), the Gothic *triu*, 'tree,' used in Greek chiefly in the sense of oak, *drŷs*. The Irish *darach*, Welsh *derw*, mean oak, and oak only. But what has to be explained here is the change of meaning from fir to oak and from oak to beech, *i.e.*, from one particular tree to another particular tree. While considering these curious changes, I happened to read Sir Charles Lyell's new work, 'The Antiquity of Man,' and I was much struck by the following passage, p. 8, *seq.* :—

"'The deposits of peat in Denmark, varying in depth from ten to thirty feet, have been formed in hollows or depressions in the Northern drift or boulder formations hereafter to be described. The lowest stratum, two or three feet thick, consists of swamp peat, composed chiefly of moss or sphagnum, above which lies another growth of peat, not made up exclusively of aquatic or swamp plants. Around the borders of the bogs, and at various depths in them, lie trunks of trees, especially of the Scotch fir (*Pinus silvestris*), often three feet in diameter, which must have grown on the margin of the peat mosses, and have frequently fallen into them. This tree is not now, nor has ever been in historical times, a native of the Danish islands, and when introduced there has not thriven; yet it was evidently indigenous in the human period, for Steenstrup has taken out with his own hands a flint instrument from below a buried trunk of one of these pines. It appears clear that the same Scotch fir was afterwards supplanted by the sessile variety of the common oak, of which many prostrate trunks occur in the peat at higher levels than the pines; and still higher the pedunculated variety of the same oak (*Quercus robur*, L.) occurs with the alder, birch (*Betula verrucosa, Ehrh.*), and hazel. The oak has in its turn been almost superseded in Denmark by the common beech.'"—*Lectures on the Science of Language,* second series, London, Longmans, 1864, p. 222 ff. ·

The conclusion which Max Müller arrives at in this way he expresses as follows:—"The fact that *phēgós* in Greek means oak, and oak only, while *fagus* in Latin, *boka* in Gothic, mean 'beech,' requires surely an explanation; and until a better one can be given, I venture to suggest that Teutonic and Italic Aryans witnessed the transition of the oak

period into the beech period, of the bronze age into
the iron age, and that while the Greeks retained
phēgós in its original sense, the Teutonic and Italian
colonists transferred the name, as an appellative, to
the new forests that were springing up in their wild
homes" (*ibid.*, p. 235).

Max Müller does not himself overlook the difficulties involved in this calling in aid of the geological periods for the explanation of the changes
in the meaning of some words. And, indeed, his
conjecture, as we shall presently see, is untenable.
The supersedure of the oak by the beech is notoriously neither an isolated occurrence in Denmark
nor a merely antediluvian one, or even altogether
an accomplished fact. It is a slow, but, it would
seem, irresistible process, observed in the latter centuries, and still going on in Germany and France.
The beech, which thrives in the shade, and, at the
same time, is capable, as Vaupell and Heyer have
shown, of depriving of light, by overshadowing, trees
requiring it, and thus bringing them to decay, dis-
places by virtue of these properties, step by step,
not only the oak, but, to a still greater extent, the
birch and pine from our woods, and finally supersedes
them. When Cæsar crossed over to Britain he did not
yet find the beech there. In the Dutch peat-bogs on
the frontiers of East Frisia stupendous wooden bridges
were discovered in 1818, which were traced back to the
expeditions of Germanicus in the first Christian century. Among the trees which had been used for these
bridges, pine and birch are found in great number,

but never beech.   Here, then, we have historical, and
not even so very remote, periods when the beech
had not yet pushed its way into countries where at
present it is quite common.   In Normandy, where
now beech forests occur more frequently than in any
other province of France, and where, on the other
hand, the pine forms, at least, no natural forests,
the submarine forests of the coasts exhibit pine, oak,
birch, elm, and hazel, but no beech.   Whereas the
latter occurs as a fossil in the Holstein moors.

As may be seen, we have not here to deal with
contrasts of sharply defined geological periods, but
with diffusion, migration, and gradual increase.   The
beech spreads from a point of Europe which must
evidently have been situated more to the south than
the coasts of the Baltic and the German Ocean, and
more to the west than the Prussian Baltic provinces,
which to this day are chiefly covered with pine and
birch.   Is the change in the meaning of its Indo-
European name connected with this migration?   In
other words, did the beech come to the Indo-Europeans
and usurp the name of the oak in the same way as
it usurped the soil of their forests ?

A simple consideration will clear up the matter
for us.   "Oak" cannot at *first* have been the meaning of beech,—"beech" is its genuine and primary
signification.   For the Romans agree with the Teutons
in the use of the word, and only the Greeks use it
in the form of *phēgós* as a name for a species of oak.
The divergence from its original use must therefore
undoubtedly be looked for among the Greeks; a

common and uniform divergence on the part of the
Romans and Teutons would be quite inexplicable.
With this the whole analogy to the palæontological
periods falls to the ground of itself, and the question
as to the connection of the change of name with the
migration of the beech must likewise be negatived.
Not that the beech came to the Indo-Europeans, nay,
not even the Indo-Europeans coming to the beech,
is the cause of the vacillation to be observed in the
words between beech and oak. We have here quite
an identical instance with the above-mentioned transfer of the name of the birch to the ash in the Latin
fraxinus. Both, it appears to me, admit of only one
interpretation. The Romans, or rather their near
Italic kindred and ancestors, populated Italy from
the North, and therewith the birch disappeared from
their view; the Greeks, advancing still farther to
the South, now no longer required the old name for
the beech. In the conception of the Italics the birch
was superseded by the ash, which, from its whitish
hue, reminded them of it, and for the Greeks a similar
oak took the place of the beech.

As to the comparison of *quercus* with *Föhre*, it is
for this very reason less safe, because in Old High
German by the side of *foraha, Föhre*, another word,
feraha, likewise occurs with the meaning of oak. The
intermediate form *percus*, which must be assumed
between *quercus* and *feraha*, points to the Greek *perkos*,
"blackish." The great part which colour plays in
the nomenclature of trees reminds us of a similar one

in the still older nomenclature of animals, and testifies to what a high degree man is an animal guided by the eye, and how everywhere language and reason grew up for him through his sight. Do we not even to this day see names of colours used with predilection in the names of trees by way of more accurate distinction, such as red beech, black poplar, white fir, or in Black Forest and the like? The common and connecting sense of *Föhre* and "oak" would accordingly be "black tree," not tree in general. Here, too, let me add that the succession of meanings assumed by Max Müller will probably have to be reversed. Oak is the original notion common to Romans and Germans, *Föhre* only the Teutonic idea. Provided the names are connected, only a partial migration of a tribe from an oak area into one of fir can have been the cause of the transfer. We meet with a quite similar instance of such a transfer: the above-mentioned *drys*, tree and oak, occurs in Lithuanic in the form of *derwa* for "pinewood," "resinous wood."

That the *pine* was known to the Indo-Europeans before their separation appears from its name, which is to be met with among the Greeks, Lithuanics, and Romans, as well as in Germany. In addition, they knew the willow, ash, alder, and hazel, but hardly any real fruit-tree; at most, perhaps, a kind of primitive apple. This, together with the demonstrable history of the beech, requires us to confine its home within somewhat narrow boundaries. The oak preponderated, as the use of the general word "tree" for "oak" among Greeks and Kelts seems to prove. The birch, too, must have had the power of vividly impressing the imagination to have been able to preserve its name almost unchanged to this day among people of such different regions; but the beech could not be greatly inferior to it, since its name was formed about the same time and in a similar way. Considering that about the beginning of the Christian era the beech had not yet advanced into Holland and England, and had in the primitive Indo-European time probably extended even far less northward, we must, I presume, proceed southward into the undisputed ancient area of that tree, which, as regards Germany, would take us about as far as the Thuringian Forest.

As regards grain-fruit, it is an established fact that in primitive times *barley* was known to the Indo-Europeans. But their knowledge of *wheat* is] in the very highest degree improbable. The Greek *zea*, "spelt," it is true, agrees with the Sanskrit and Zend *javas;* but this happens to be barley, and the derivative *javasa* means herbage for fodder, the Lithuanic *jawas* generally corn. Among the Ossets in the Caucasus *jau* is millet. Of the highest importance, on the contrary, is the acquaintance with *rye* on the part of the Indo-Europeans, and the remarkable divergence in the meaning of this name in their present various abodes. By means of Grimm's and Pictet's comparisons it has been ascertained that the Sanskrit word *vrîhi*, "rice," is in reality identical with *Roggen*, "rye," Lithuanic *ruggys*, Russian *rosh*, and

K

that the significations fluctuate between the two kinds of grain according to the climatic variation. Our word *Reiss*, "rice," is, in the first instance, derived from the French *riz;* this from the Greek *oryza,* which in its turn must have been borrowed from the Persian word for the Indian *vrîhi.* *Reiss,* therefore, is a word of foreign origin. That, however, not only Slavonians, Lithuanians, and Germans participated in the meaning "rye," but that even the ancient Thracians had the word *briza* for it, is a most remarkable circumstance, to which I shall return in the sequel, and which proves that the meaning of "rice" was merely Indo-Persian, and "rye" the real primary signification. An area in which rye and barley, and not also wheat, thrive, is, perhaps, to be found only in Northern Europe; but with reference to a very early time we must, doubtless, exclude even a somewhat more southerly zone from the culture of wheat.

Before I quit this line of argument, by which I am endeavouring to establish my proposition on botanical grounds, and pass on to another series of arguments, I must mention a plant which has escaped both Pictet and the author of the "Wörterbuch der Indogermanischen Grundsprache" ("Dictionary of the Original Indo-Germanic Language"), and the occurrence of which among the primitive Indo-Europeans may, for various reasons, claim a high share of interest on our part. It is the *woad,* a genuine European dye-weed, which, in more recent times, owing to the importation of indigo, has in a great measure lost its importance. The word is of ancient Indo-European origin; and though, for intelligible reasons, it is not to be met with in Sanskrit, the Greek, Latin, and German forms are sufficient evidence of the fact. In Greek, the name of the plant is *isatis* or *isate;* in Latin, *vitrum.* Its real name in Greek, however, must have been *visatis,* and, as happened in all the words in which the *v* occurred, it must have lost this sound. The German *Waid* is derived from *waisd,* as the medieval Latin forms *waisda, wesdia, guaisdium,* old French *guesde,* now *guède,* show. Accordingly we shall have to assume that *vitrum* too comes from *vistrum.* The Gauls called the plant *glastum* or *guastum. Glas* signifies in the Keltic languages blue, green, grey; and the striking agreement of this *glas* with our *Glas* (glass), while the Latin *vitrum* signifies both woad and glass, has been already explained very correctly by Diefenbach in such a way that both objects may have received their names from their bluish colour. We must here remember that glass was originally by no means colourless; the earliest was probably green. The leaves of the woad plant (provided these, not perhaps the sap, were regarded in giving it a name) are likewise light blue-green, and the syllable *vis* must in the first instance have signified to the Indo-Europeans the green colour, which, however, was not sharply distinguished either from the blue or from the grey. To compare with it the Latin *viridis,* green, does not cause the least etymological difficulty : *idis* is a termination which is generally *idus,* and as such occurs in many adjectives descriptive of colours, *e.g., pallidus,* pale.

That *s* between vowels in Latin often changes into *r* is a well-known fact; the root of *viridis* then is *vis*. But now, at a somewhat later period, blue objects too were designated by words from this root, especially some flowers. It is more than probable that the Greek name of the violet, *ion*, is derived from *vion*, and this again from *vison*. The Romans formed *viola* out of *vion* by appending a diminutive syllable; and from the Latin word again our *Veilchen* (violet) is derived. The Hindoos designated another blue flower by the same name, *visha - pushpa*, the "visa - flower" (for *sh* occurs here, according to a well-known phonetic law in Sanscrit, instead of *s*). *Visinî*, too, is the blue lotos. On the other hand, *vishada* is green vitriol, which reminds us that our *Vitriol* too is equally derived from the above-mentioned Latin *vitrum*. But originally *visa* signified every turbid fluid; hence *visha* in Sanskrit, *virus* in Latin, *ios* in Greek, mean *poison, venom, drivel*. The Greek word also implies *rust*, which the language conceives as *dirt*. From the notion of "turbid fluid" the word was transferred to the "dyeing fluid," which at first needed not necessarily be green or blue: in Sanskrit *viçada* even means "white."

The foregoing deductions may perhaps appear too minute, but connected as they are with the question as to how far the primitive age already distinguished blue from green, they could not well be passed over. But what may have inspired the Indo-Europeans at that remote period with such a lively interest in the woad plant to make use of a colour-term, otherwise scarcely familiar to them, for its appellation ? No other plant besides bearing a name in common with it from the root *vis*, the woad must have been the real " blue flower " of the primitive time, the prototype of the violet and lotos flower. Now, was it perhaps the " paintings " of the Indo-Europeans which made the woad plant important to them, or did they already, like classical antiquity, dye their woollen stuffs with it ? An interesting fact which several ancient writers report to us leaves no doubt on the subject. It concerns the Britons. Cæsar, Pliny, and Pomponius Mela testify to us that it was their own body which the ancient Britons used to paint with woad. According to Pliny, " the British women, on certain festive days, used to paint the whole body with Gallic *glastum*, imitating the colour of the Ethiopians." Cæsar says " all the Britons painted themselves blue (cæruleum) with woad (*vitro*), and they looked all the more terrible for it in battle." Pomponius says " it is uncertain whether the Britons painted their bodies with woad for the purpose of ornament or for some other reason." If this British custom, which was doubtless a religious rite, presents a wonderful parallel to that of the Indians in the New World, reliable testimonies are not lacking that the Britons regularly tattooed themselves. In the same way as this practice recurs on the whole earth, they drew figures on their skins by needle-pricks, which were then painted over with a dye (atramento) (Isidorus, Hisp. Or. ix. 2., 103, and xx. See Diefenbach, Orig. eur. s. v. Britones). Herodian states they did not clothe themselves on purpose to let the figures on the skin be seen, and wore scarcely anything but iron hoops round the neck and body. According to Cæsar, however, they clothed themselves in skins of animals. Petersen has recently directed attention to reports about cannibalism in Britain so late as in the fifth century of the Christian era. On comparing the barbarous condition of those earliest Indo-European inhabitants of the British Isles with the comparatively great culture of their near relatives, the Gauls, it is impossible to account for that condition by a retrogression. Supposing the Kelts populating Britain had found there non-Indo-European savage aborigines, yet the influence of these on a superior people would nevertheless not have sufficed to depress it to their low level, any more than it gave up its language. On the other hand, it is well known that the first cause of all cultural progress of the Gauls was the establishment of the Greek colony at Marseilles about 600 before Christ.

It is truly astonishing how from every spot on which a Greek foot stepped culture spread abroad. The Gauls owed to Greek influence the start they had of the Teutons throughout ancient times. The Gauls learned from the Greeks the alphabet, and in their turn taught it to the Teutons, whose Runes have thus originated; and altogether the civilisation of the Teutons increased in proportion as they intercommunicated with the Gauls. Subsequently the Gauls eagerly received Roman culture, and the influence, not always rated at its proper value, which France of old, and nearly at all times, exercised

on German literature, science, and mode of life, is due
to her early and unbroken connection with ancient
Southern culture. What, however, was the condition
of the Kelts before their contact with these civilising
influences, that of the Britons evidently represents in
the most unadulterated manner, though even here some
deductions will have to be made, as the intercourse with
the Kelts of the Continent continued brisk, and according to Cæsar, *e.g.*, besides iron, brass served as money,
though the latter metal was not indigenous in the
island, but imported. As to the climate, in Britain it
was not of a nature from which one might expect a
brutalising influence ; on the contrary, it was milder
there than in Gaul, which was in bad repute among
the Romans for its cold. Evidently the barbarous
inhabitants of Britain present to us the original stage
of Keltic culture, and we shall certainly not be inclined
to presuppose in these savage Kelts a highly civilised
Aryan people, which, on its farther migrations, was
degraded to the level of tattooed savages, but surely
deem it more probable that it is the wholly unmodified,
most embryonic forms of the Indo-European nature
which we find left here in the North. And if the
above-mentioned fair-skinned man represented in the
tomb-chambers of King Sethos is really an Indo-European, and, in that case, of course, by far the earliest
Indo-European individual we know of, his representation quite agrees with such conceptions, seeing that he
is likewise tattooed. To all appearance the Britons
emigrated at a very early date from Gaul to their

island, and most faithfully preserved the character of their native stock on the primitive level which it occupied at the time of their emigration. This opinion is favoured by the religious importance which Britain, according to Cæsar's statement, had for the Gauls of the Continent, who sent their sons to the Druidical school there, where they had to learn many thousands of holy verses; a circumstance which is scarcely conceivable without an ancient venerable seat of the priesthood; nay, which might even permit us to conclude to re-immigrated British colonies into Gaul, who considered the intercourse with the British Druids as a connection with their original home.

The presumption that the primitive Indo-European stock was of Northern origin is likewise in perfect agreement with what language reveals to us as to the climatic conditions. The common vocabulary shows us snow and ice, winter and spring, but not summer and autumn. The deep and permanent impression which the cold of the winter must have made on that people has not escaped Pictet. For this reason, too, he chooses among the Southern countries, where he considers himself bound to place that stock, the coldest and bleakest. But this is evidently inconsistent; and if we consider the matter without prejudice, we must not, in the first instance, think of a cold climate that owes its nature to its mountains or some local accident, but of a Northern one. Pictet mentions the three seasons, spring, summer, and winter, known by the Vedic Hindoos, and also quotes Tacitus' statement that the

Germans had ideas and words (*intellectum et vocabula*) for winter, spring, and summer, but that the name of autumn was as unknown to them as its gifts. By reason of this remarkable passage alone I presume we may say: If the home of the primitive Indo-Europeans was not Germany, it must, at least, as regards the temperature and impression of the seasons, have fully resembled the Germany as Tacitus still knew it. The assumption of a temperate but still frosty climate agrees also with the poverty of the Indo-European languages in common names for insects. Thus the spider, for instance, has no ancient name (unless we would compare together the Russian *pauk* and the Cymrian *copyn*, Anglo-Saxon *coppa*, English *cob ;* for *aranea* is only borrowed from the Greek *arachne*), and the bug, too, spared those patriarchs of Europe. Ants, gadflies, and gnats were extant among them. The mammalia which they indubitably knew are the ox, sheep, pig, horse, stag, and dog; the bear, wolf, mouse, badger (Greek *trochos*), and probably the fox too. That they were not acquainted with the jackal is tolerably certain. The *beaver* and the *viverra*, of which latter word it is difficult to decide if it originally meant the martin, ferret, weasel, or squirrel, are also interesting. The Greeks, among whom it signifies squirrel, have corrupted the name into *skiuros*, which seems to imply "shadow-tail." This is only a specimen of the well-known word-disfigurement by popular etymology, which has peculiarly affected this word. In passing on from Greek to Latin and then to French it assumed the forms *sciurulus, écureuil,* and the French form has given birth to our *Eichhorn,* as well as to a series of other disfigurements already met with in the old Teutonic dialects. Of our word *Katze* (cat) it is not certain either if it was not used for weasel, in the same way as *felis* vacillates between the same double meaning. The earliest form of *Katze* is most faithfully preserved in the Ossetic *gado,* and this is probably identical with the Greek *galee,* weasel or cat. Among the species of birds, which to all appearance were numerous, let me mention only, by way of selecting those about which we are most certain, the vulture, the raven, the starling, the wild goose, and the duck; the pigeon was most likely not known. There existed a general word for worm, and equally so one for serpent. The otter and the eel were known, but no other name of a fish seems to be found, nor any common word for shell. There is no denying that a consideration of this circumstance must tend considerably to shake the assumption that the primitive Indo-Europeans were familiar with the sea. The mere existence of a word for sea cannot by any means prove such familiarity, as any inland people of some degree of activity, and not living wholly excluded from intercourse with the outer world, must come to hear something of the existence of the sea. To this must be added that the Indo-Europeans have not even an expression properly and exclusively signifying the sea. *Meer* (sea) not only means also lake, but, moreover, even moor, morass. Nor does there exist an ancient Indo-European word for "salt." In the words for "wave" all the branches of language differ. The *Sund* (sound) of the northern seas reappears in Sanskrit as *sindhu* (stream), and has there become the proper name of the Indus, and for us, after the example of the Persians, even that of India. Even for the *oyster* the inhabitants of the coasts of the German Ocean had to borrow a Greek name. Finally, the primitive Indo-Europeans in their navigation used the oar indeed, but no sails; and yet, if they had lived by the sea, these could hardly have remained unknown to them. Of metals they knew gold; far less certain are we as to silver in the earliest time. Their acquaintance with iron is scarcely to be doubted, as the agreement between the German, Sanskrit, and Zend here speaks quite plainly; but I doubt whether they knew brass or copper, for the agreement between the Latin *æs* and the Gothic *ais* may easily arise from the Goths having borrowed the Latin word; and the Greek *chalkos* means, indeed, in Hómer copper, and not till Pindar also iron. But as a cognate word in Russian means only iron, and the Greek *chalkis* is also the name of a *black* bird, I still think iron to be the older notion, which was only subsequently transferred to another metal. Other metals than gold and iron, and perhaps silver and brass, were not known to the primitive Indo-Europeans; nor were they acquainted with precious stones or pearls.

I must here break off, reserving a farther series of arguments for a later dissertation. If what I have hitherto brought forward should let the proposition that the primitive Indo-European people had its home in Germany still appear hypothetical—if, perhaps, we should not succeed at all in attaining absolute certainty on so difficult a question—I beg, on the other hand, the reader may calmly consider what arguments are really extant in favour of the conception hitherto current, and that, at the worst, hypothesis would only be opposed to hypothesis. At first the source of the mighty stream of peoples that poured down over half a world was looked for on the remote south-eastern frontier, and then, urged by weighty arguments, it was moved back only as far as was indispensably necessary. But as no point of the earth in this respect has any right of being preferred to another, a compromise is in no way better than a totally opposite view. Meanwhile only one of the two opposite hypotheses is supported by arguments; for as to the migration from the east, no evidence has ever been adduced in its favour. He, therefore, that eschews hypotheses must at least be just, and be satisfied not to know aught on the present question. But if he is inclined to give the preference to either hypothesis, I believe he will have to give it to that which is comparatively best established, even though the arguments should not yet suffice for a final decision.

PRINTED BY BALLANTYNE, HANSON AND CO.
EDINBURGH AND LONDON